Beyond All Boundaries

Book 3: Interdimensional Worlds

Lyn Willmott

Library of Congress Cataloging-in-Publication Data

Beyond All Boundaries Book 3: Interdimensional Worlds by Lyn Willmott -1938-

As the story moves into the last book of the trilogy, we know that Chaldee's kingdom has been destroyed, meaning she must seek a new homeland, but the search seem fruitless until.

1. Spiritual 2. Interdimensional 3. Earthlings 4. Metaphysical
I. Willmott, Lyn, 1938 II. Metaphysical III. Interdimensional IV. Title

Library of Congress Catalog Card Number: 2021949873
ISBN: 9781950639045

Cover Art and Layout: Victoria Cooper Art
Book set in: Times New Roman, Century Schoolbook
Book Design: Summer Garr

Published by:

PO Box 754, Huntsville, AR 72740
800-935-0045 or 479-738-2348; fax 479-738-2448
WWW.OZARKMT.COM

Printed in the United States of America

Dedicated to my granddaughters:

Sophie and Pippa Mills

Contents

Part One
Searching for a New Home

Chapter One
Back Again

Joe stood motionless, astounded by his recollection. He remembered standing on this very spot just over two years ago, gazing down into Chaldee's kingdom minutes after that alarming eruption. It had not been a waterfall at that point, just a chaotic frenzy of rock and dust. Much had happened since then; a catalyst that had turned his world inside out. Now he was back again, this time leading Chaldee's people as they searched for a new home.

With a deep sigh, Joe returned to the present, quietly assisting his small group of explorers to make camp above the waterfall. He had suggested they stay here overnight and prepare for tomorrow's climb back down into the valley. As he sensed their disappointment, he had assured everyone that by tomorrow afternoon they would be back at the caves.

Later, as Joe lay back staring up into a night enriched by stars, he had to admit he was feeling disappointed by their journey into the Kimberley; it was quite obvious, these people did not share his love of country, nor did they have any idea of how many thousands of years his ancestors had lived here, had become "one" with the land. Of course, this was why he cared so much for its stark, dry beauty, but this expedition had revealed that what he loved had appalled Chaldee's people, so tomorrow morning, they would leave this arid splendor and return to their valley.

These falls appeared after Rod's courageous undertaking had realigned Chaldee's community with the outside world. The river forming the falls was only a trickle of water right now, but the climb was still perilous. They needed the clear light of morning to safely manage the descent, and although he wished they could remain out here, he knew these wonderful people had been used to a cool, very sheltered lifestyle. They did not want to put down roots in his world. Even Enka, his right-hand man, had refused to consider what Joe was proposing. This meant that Chaldee would have to seek another solution as to where they would settle. It concerned him deeply, because he had grown fond of them and he wondered what their future held.

Joe also worried about what lay ahead for his human kinsmen. Today, as he pushed through the familiar terrain, he could feel a change, almost as if the planet was speaking. Over the past few years, there had been terrible bushfires, droughts, floods, and a pandemic, causing Joe to feel that something new was beginning to occur. With his heightened senses, he felt as if this "time" was almost at an end and looming just beyond them was quite a different world. He was not sure if it was due to the sun, or whether it was the Earth itself, but he could feel a different energy simmering across the land. Although he could sense it, he was not confident enough to pinpoint the change; nevertheless, he would certainly tell Chaldee tomorrow. She needed to factor in everything if she was going to make the right move for her people.

Wearily, Chaldee leaned against the barricade, lost in the hush of the fading day. She had been hoping for another telepathic message from Joe. He had reached her earlier in the day, but his communication was so muddled she was left wondering if something was amiss.

The entire community depended on the outcome of Joe's search party. He had chosen to take Enka and a handful of the more adventurous villagers with him, looking at the possibility of establishing a new kingdom out in the wilds of the Kimberley Ranges. When they had not returned today, she had reached out to Joe, telepathically asking about his progress and from what she could glean the expedition had not been a success. Nevertheless, it seemed she must wait until the group returned in order to have a clearer understanding of the problem.

Chaldee found a seat on her favorite rock at the edge of the makeshift patio. This structure was like a balcony overlooking the valley and was built to hide the entrance to the caves. Chaldee could often be found here pondering her people's future, trying to make sense out of what her next move should be. Tonight, her mood was grim. She knew that time was short, that her people had to move out of the caves soon for their standard of life was so bad that cracks were starting to appear in their well-being. She remembered the lushness of her forest home before Rod's unification and the almost sacred ability she had to step between the worlds because of her palace's magical environment.

As she gazed out into the darkening valley, Chaldee was pleased she could not see the wreckage of the palace for this marked the end of a most treasured period in her life. It hurt to remember those wondrous days when she would ride out into the forest often ending up at Beech's Quarter. The old Beech Myrtle tree was the wisest mind in the forest, and she missed his counsel. Perhaps tomorrow she should take time away from the cave life and pay him a visit. If she could seek his advice, it might lift the weight from her heart. Chaldee sighed, reminding herself that the past must be forgotten for the wonder of those days ended completely when Rod altered the energy field and aligned the two realities.

These days, existence was very solid and very serious. As her mind continued to wander back across the events that had led to these caves, Chaldee recalled how the Oracle had supported her during those drastic and exacting times. When leaders from many countries had gathered in Sydney for a special meeting, his counsel had been invaluable. She had tried to warn those businessmen and politicians of the coming Earth changes, desperately reaching out to their dark minds, but even as the confrontation was taking place the Oracle told her they were rejecting her message. Despite that failure and also the joy of meeting Paul, the relief she felt as she returned to this valley washed away all frustration; but in reality, there was no home to return to. Her palace had been destroyed, as had most of her precious belongings. Indeed, existence here was becoming tortuous, even though her people had worked hard to create a regal space for her in the caves. They had wanted to fashion a place worthy of a leader and she loved her secluded, tranquil cubbyhole. They had enriched her space with a few personal treasures, saved during that terrible day of destruction. In this private retreat, the cavern roof was so high the air often emitted magical tremors during her meditations. She smiled a little now as she realized that her people had indeed given her a heartfelt reminder of the past splendors of her kingdom—so all had not been lost.

A little later when Paul joined her, Chaldee felt her anxiety ease slightly. Although he did not break the silence, she knew he was also concerned about their predicament. Indeed, he had already proposed that they search deeper into the cave system. He had spoken about the hidden world of Agartha, a land of myth that the Tibetan Buddhists claimed was an inner-Earth society; explaining that in their history, Shambhala was a mysterious wonder, a mystical city found deep inside the planet. Chaldee had not scoffed, although she had quickly put an end to Paul's proposal to go searching for such an unknown place. What he was suggesting sounded too outlandish, too dangerous; nevertheless, she knew this would not be the end of the conversation. When Paul put forward an idea, it usually came to pass.

"It's very quiet tonight," she whispered.

"Feels edgy … as if the Earth is making preparations for something."

Chaldee's look was sharp. "What do you mean?"

"I'm not sure … makes me feel uneasy, Chaldee, as if something is approaching," Paul said thoughtfully.

"I may know of what you speak."

Paul's smile was a little ironic. "If I can feel it, I'm sure you can, too."

Chaldee looked at him closely. As an Earthling, Paul did not have quite the same ability to move up through the layers of consciousness as she did, yet he seemed to have some sort of awareness. "What do you sense?"

"I don't know, Chaldee. I've had this feeling before … maybe it was why I joined the protest movement in the first place, but since being up here with you it has grown stronger. I feel these times have become very dangerous."

"I have heard that some of your scientists speak of a coming catastrophe."

Paul shook his head. "I really don't think it will be that drastic … but it has something to do with the planet."

"I also feel this, but we must wait. If we are to be warned, then hopefully it will be given in time."

Paul sighed helplessly. "Are you saying somehow you will be given information? When will I ever get used to you, Chaldee?" He draped his arm across her shoulders and for a few moments they stood in silence.

Looking out, feeling the dark depth of the night, Chaldee smiled hesitantly. "Maybe we are just caught up in the death of the day."

"No, it's more than that," Paul grunted. "More than whatever is coming … no, what I'm also trying to deal with has to do with what you just said … about you being given information … it makes me feel a bit dumb."

Chaldee was startled. Then as he turned to face her, she picked up his thoughts and realized how awkward and uneasy he was feeling. "Paul, I don't understand!"

"I guess it's just me … but I must admit I'm a bit miffed." Paul paused, thoughtfully staring into her eyes. "It's as if I have to learn who you are all over again. Things were different while we were helping Professor Egeland."

Chaldee brushed her fingers against his mouth. "I know! And I am so sorry. My people expect me to behave in a certain way."

"Yes, I understand," Paul said quickly. "And it's okay … I guess I just need time." He shrugged slightly then moved closer, drawing her hands up to his chest. Chaldee dropped her head on his shoulder, and they stood locked in an uneasy silence.

She was very concerned by his hesitancy but had no idea how to reassure him for their differences seem to have been dramatically emphasized since they had returned from Sydney. She was the leader of her people, and although Paul knew this, he was struggling to adjust.

Eventually Paul moved away. "You seem preoccupied … has Joe been in touch?"

She gave a slight nod. "Yes, it was very jumbled, but he seemed … negative, I think you would say. Apparently, the area out there beyond this valley is far too hot and too barren for my people."

"Makes sense … after the world you guys have always known."

"I am sorry I am so distant, though. It's because I'm quite concerned."

Paul did not answer, and they stood at the barrier to the caves silently gazing out into the darkness, aware of the land, of the night calls and the uncertainty of their future.

It was around daybreak when Joe snapped awake, shaken by a loud, mechanical roar. For a few seconds he felt disorientated, not sure why he was hearing helicopters, then with a yell of realization he hurriedly woke the others, telling them to quickly hide among the boulders. Then wriggling on his stomach Joe moved out into the area just above the falls, listening to the change in the motor's sound, straining to see what was happening. It appeared they had landed somewhere quite close, but there was no sign of them, no rising dust nor sound of voices. He wondered how many helicopters had landed, but even more important how many soldiers were out there scouring the area. Were they still looking for evidence of Professor Egeland's research? As far as Joe knew the authorities still had no idea of the interdimensional qualities of the professor's powder. But then maybe they were just checking the wreckage that was once Chaldee's palace—that would make sense. The authorities would still be searching for evidence, bodies, paraphernalia, anything that might help them learn more about Chaldee's race and their whereabouts. Joe knew the military had returned a few times since the attack, and now they were back again, many months later! He frowned as he mulled it over. Were they looking for Chaldee's hideout?

Enka joined him and they stared down through the

dense bush. "What is it, Joe? Why would the soldiers come back?"

Joe shrugged, wishing he had brought the binoculars. "Whatever it is, we are in trouble," he muttered. "If we're caught, or even if they see us, the caves might be discovered."

"We better tell the others."

"Right," Joe whispered as he crawled back to the group now sheltered under a large outcrop of rock. "We might have to stay here a while, folks; preserve your water because it could be some time before those guys down there decide to leave."

They all nodded silently. Joe was pleased by their self-restraint. This was one reason why he enjoyed living among these people. They were steady, committed, and loyal, and he knew they would persevere with the heat and the dust for as long as he asked. Then, just as Joe was sliding back to the edge of the waterfall, he heard gunfire, two quick shots that split the air.

"Joe," Enka called urgently. "What was that?"

Before Joe could answer, there was a gliding flutter of wings as the chief crow and three of his flock noisily landed on the rocks near him. Although Joe had worked with these huge black birds once before, he was still in awe of his newly acquired psychic abilities. To be able to understand the language of these crows and to exchange information with them was priceless, especially right now.

"We have just witnessed the Commander's demise," the chief crow squawked.

"The Commander!" Enka's eyes widened in horror.

"Who?" Joe demanded, feeling agitated.

"The Commander was the head of our army. He caused the uprising," Enka explained. "Princess Chaldee had him imprisoned, but he escaped when the palace was destroyed."

Joe nodded, turning back to the crows. "And you

saw this?"

"Just now. We saw the Commander use his power," squawked the chief crow.

"He used much power," another bird agreed.

"He stunned two of the soldiers before they used those long weapons on him," squawked another.

"And he fell. They use dangerous and cruel weapons, Master Joe," the chief crow complained.

Joe sat cross-legged in the dust, shocked not only by the sudden appearance of the crows but by the story they were telling. "I can't believe you saw this … have you been watching us, too?"

"We watch all movement. We saw the Commander enter the valley two days ago." All the birds bobbed their heads in agreement as their chief went on: "We think he was trying to reach Chaldee."

"Do you mean telepathically?"

"Yes, Master Joe. But she must have denied him because he seemed not to know what to do or where to go," the chief crow said aggressively. "Chaldee was right to cast him out."

The rest of the group had now gathered around Joe and the crows.

"It was the Commander who tried to turn us against each other," said one woman.

"You are right, Shorna." Enka was nodding. "It was dangerous and ill-timed."

"It was the start of where we are now," Shorna said sadly.

"Yes, but it was the blue orbs that caused the Commander's downfall," another voice piped up. "They filled the air with their presence."

"We saw this, too," croaked the chief crow in awe. "We saw those amazing orbs in the sky."

"They eliminated the Shadows, that's why the caves we are in are now safe," Enka said, turning to Joe attempting to help him absorb some of their history.

Although Joe was curious, especially at the mention of flying orbs, his mind was still focused on the soldiers in the valley below. "You can fill me in on this whole uprising thing later, guys. Right now we need to know how many soldiers are down there and what they are doing."

The chief crow nodded as he silently assessed what he had seen. "There are two of those machines and eleven or twelve humans—but because of the Commander's power two are now unconscious and have been taken to one of the machines. The Commander hurt them badly so it will be hours before they wake. The Commander has also been put into a machine, so they must be going to take him with them."

"So, we are facing at least ten soldiers, all armed ..."

"With thick clothing and strange masks," the chief crow cut in.

"Combat troops," Joe said thoughtfully. "They are not messing around this time!"

"Should I let the Princess know, Joe?" Enka asked.

"Yeah ... do that ... but say the crows are with us and we have a plan."

"Do we?" the chief crow squawked doubtfully. "What is this mysterious plan?"

"Yeah ... well ... we'll think of something ... let's not alarm her. Things are bad enough."

Enka nodded in agreement and began to telepathically reach out to his Princess.

In the caves, the morning meeting was just starting. The Master Speaker had prepared an agenda, and Chaldee was about to list the day's chores when the muffled sound of helicopters could be heard.

"They're back," Paul growled.

"Not another invasion … surely not." Chaldee hurried to the cave entrance and carefully moving the sliding rock-like partition she stepped out into the cool morning air. Immediately she could see where the two helicopters had landed. It was just to one side of what used to be the palace complex. Shading her eyes, she saw a swarm of perhaps ten soldiers. Frowning and now greatly concerned, Chaldee watched as they spread out over the rubble. Obviously, they had been instructed to search for more evidence.

Suddenly Chaldee was shocked to see another figure emerge from the trees; as she saw two soldiers collapse in front of this stranger, she realized it was the outcast Commander, the renegade leader who had almost taken control of her people and who had escaped at the time of the human onslaught. Angrily, she watched him, wondering what he wanted with the humans. Then there was the ugly sound of gunfire and she saw the Commander falling forward. Chaldee watched in horror as two soldiers grabbed the wounded man by the arms and dragged him over to a helicopter. What would the human authorities do to him? Even though Chaldee had banished him from her kingdom, she loathed seeing the Commander treated so badly. As she continued to watch, she saw these same men load the two unconscious soldiers into the other helicopter. It would be hours before they regained their senses—but those soldiers down there would have no idea what they were dealing with. Chaldee watched for a few more minutes, wondering when they would leave and whether they had found anything in the debris, then with a deep sigh she crept back inside.

"We heard gunfire, Your Highness," said a very worried Master Speaker.

"Yes, Zell," she nodded, then turned her attention to the meeting. "The humans are again searching through what is left of the palace. I am positive they are looking for clues to where we might be." Chaldee paused, unsure of how to tell them who had just been captured. "The gunfire you heard was aimed at our Commander. He has been wounded and they have placed him in one of their machines."

There was a collective gasp as they heard the Commander's name mentioned. He had been a fearful presence when he ruled the army, but now as they heard Chaldee's words, they were shocked by the news that the Earthlings had taken him.

A sudden agitated turbulence in the cave alerted Chaldee to their concern. How much more would her people have to suffer? She looked at Paul but could see he was not aware of their stress, but Zell, her Master Speaker, was. The idea of one of their people being taken away by humans was alarming. Although they had all come to know Paul, had accepted him as her suitor, and they knew Joe well enough to feel he was a part of the community, they still despised the Earthling race.

As she probed the surrounding atmosphere, Chaldee felt the delicate impulse of another mind gently meeting hers. Immediately she realized Enka was telepathically reaching out to her. With a slight movement of her hand, she silenced the meeting. Momentarily, she turned her attention inward. Enka was confirming what she had seen and was suggesting that Joe had a plan. Quickly she cut across his thoughts, warning him that their group must remain hidden. They must not engage these humans in any type of conflict. It was imperative that the soldiers not be aware of their presence. She repeated the warning and was pleased when Enka confirmed her instructions.

"Everybody, Joe and his group are caught at the top of the rockfall. They, like us, must remain out of sight.

Soldiers have captured the Commander and I have no idea what he might tell them, but he knows nothing of our whereabouts, and it must remain so."

"This Commander guy might know something," Paul interjected. "Remember, the authorities want all of us … and they especially want you, Chaldee."

"Of course." Chaldee smiled slightly as she looked across at Paul. "I wish we had some way of contacting Jake in Sydney. He may be able to find out what these militant warmongers intend to do with the Commander."

"It's a pity Jake refused your help," Paul said. "He objected, not because he doubted you but because he regarded your abilities as beyond him."

Chaldee smiled briefly. "He did seem very skeptical, whereas Adele embraced our world, and was becoming quite skilled at using her telepathic ability. She seemed to understand that everyone can become telepathic."

Paul cocked his head on one side, as if about to argue. Instead, he said thoughtfully: "But she's showing her documentary in the UK, and Jake's working on ways to distribute the professor's powder, so they are both quite busy. I doubt if they would think anything else would be happening here," Paul sighed despondently. "We really are off the radar, aren't we?"

"What about Master Ben, Your Highness?" Zell asked.

Chaldee nodded to her Master Speaker, acknowledging to herself how this wonderful man was so positive, so supportive. He was always trying to help. "Apparently Ben is using his helicopter, flying for some mining company in western Australia," she said.

"He had a six-month contract," Paul cut in. "We won't see him for another few weeks, I'm afraid."

"There does not seem to be an answer," Chaldee said quietly. "But right now, we need to concentrate on what is happening outside. I have no idea how long Joe and our people will have to remain hidden, but we can only send them positive energy." She glanced at one of the palace guards. "I would like you to stand watch outside. We need to know exactly what these soldiers do, and where they go."

The guard nodded silently, saluting as he followed orders.

Chaldee felt the atmosphere becoming calm and was relieved that her people seemed a little more settled.

"Then let us begin the meeting," the Master Speaker said quietly, and their attention turned to the more mundane matters.

❋ ❋ ❋

Joe's team spent most of the morning sheltering under the rocky outcrop, then as the sun reached high into the sky, they heard the roar of the helicopters.

"They're leaving," Joe shouted. He inched over to the edge of the rockfall, watching as both helicopters lifted into the air, turning south. "I thought they would have stayed much longer."

"They had injured men," Enka reminded him.

Joe nodded, watching until the helicopters disappeared. "Okay … I guess it is safe to go!"

Happily, Joe led the way down the precarious cliff face and the group hurried back through the valley to the caves.

Chaldee met them at the entrance. "I'm glad you are all back safely." Smiling, she embraced each one, then turned to Joe. "You must rest."

"No, it's important we give our report—we can rest later." Joe looked at Enka for conformation.

"We have much to discuss, Madame. It is important

that everybody hears what we have to say," Enka agreed.

Joe was pleased to see that Chaldee understood. He watched as she called everybody together. The group assembled in the main cave and as they organized the seating, he came forward, sending out a calming energy. "Please, if everybody can relax. We have much to tell you, but it is Enka who should speak, for he understands your needs much better than I do." Joe stepped back, allowing Enka to lead the meeting.

"As most of you know, we have spent the last few days scouting around the area out beyond this valley," Enka began, recapping on their history as he tried to find a way to tell the people of his disappointment. "Now that the kingdom has been realigned, our world has vanished, and I know we all regard the time we are spending here in these caves as a breathing space between our loss and the new direction we must all take." Enka glanced over at Joe, shrugging helplessly.

Joe stood up, waving at Enka to sit. Although he did not really want to be the bringer of bad news, he could see Enka's unease. "It was hoped that this foray into the wilderness would give us a way forward."

Joe paused as Thara cut in. "The land beyond this place is harsh. It is hot and seems very barren compared to the world we have always known."

"Thara is right … we could not survive out there," Shorna called out almost in defiance. She was standing at the back of the meeting and all heads turned as she continued. "It is an arid, parched landscape. It would overwhelm all of us within days. Believe me, we cannot consider moving there."

"But where else can we go?"

Within seconds the meeting had fallen into shambles with people calling out, crying, some even begging for a positive direction. Joe raised his hands, calling for calm. "Shorna is giving us one view, but I know that if we found an area with water …"

"No," Enka cut across his words. "No, Joe, we cannot move my people out into such a hostile environment. It's out of the question."

"I seem to have a past life memory that might be helpful," Shorna called out. "It is almost like a whisper … a dream perhaps." She hesitated, seeming to try to find the best way to describe her images. "Yesterday while we were out in that heat, suddenly I felt I had been here before, aeons ago, when I was part of a different civilization."

The room grew quiet as they began to listen, then someone called out: "Atlantis?"

"No … no. Older than that. Maybe Lemurian. I'm not sure. We were a small community … it was as remote then as it is now, but the area was plentiful back then, with small water holes, lakes, greenery, and many types of animals. We were on the edge of our civilization, living in a large stone building. It was a place of learning; very strong, very safe so we felt secure even though we were so far away from the center of our world … which felt … ah … felt to be a long way away. Perhaps across a vast stretch of water … though I'm not sure. Strangely, what was happening to me then seems very much like what is happening now … as if I am repeating an experience." Shorna paused, quite overcome by what she was relating. "There were perhaps twenty of us, all dressed in rough blue robes. We ate very little, and our energy or frequency was vastly different to what it is now. That was why we were in this earthly place, to learn to align our frequency; to become more grounded, more solid. The Earth itself was helping." Shorna gulped back a sob, her voice full of wonder. "The Earth was holding us steady, helping with our meditations." She stopped, overcome by emotion.

"How strange, I remember such a time of expansion," Enka said softly. "A time when we were part of each other and could feel our combined energy field, and we, too, were learning how to manage our frequency."

"It was long ago." Shorna sniffed back her tears. "Many lifetimes have passed, many time-slips have occurred since then, but as I stood in that massive landscape yesterday, the Earth itself seemed to hold this memory."

Enka nodded, looking around. "Does Shorna's story remind anyone else of a past life?"

Joe nodded slowly. "I'm not very clear about these things, but it feels right, especially about the changes in the land." He paused. "When we were out there yesterday, I got the feeling that this land was once plentiful but has been turning into desert for a very long time."

"As the planet becomes warmer," Thara whispered.

Despondently, Chaldee gazed around at her people. She had been listening to the memories of past lives, but it did not soothe her worries of the present. "Then it seems we must alter our plan to find a new settlement."

Joe's face mirrored Chaldee's unhappiness.

"Perhaps we could investigate my idea," Paul interrupted. "We could consider exploring this cave complex. I know it goes a long way back, and I think there might be a few tunnels leading even farther inward."

Joe suddenly grinned. They had already discussed Paul's idea, and it would certainly give the group another viewpoint.

"I feel the risk might be too great," Chaldee murmured.

"Yeah … but now is the time to talk about it. We need to move forward," Paul said eagerly.

Chapter Two
The Commander's Capture

The Commander had been surprised by the arrival of these raucous human machines. He had only seen such contraptions once before, when they attacked the palace and destroyed his kingdom, now they were back, but for what reason? Occasionally, in his long life the Commander had encountered humans, but always they had accidently strayed into his world and were quickly sent back into their own reality, usually unconscious with little memory of what they had found, but these Earthlings were far more aggressive. He was intrigued by both the strange bulky armor they were wearing and the long weapons they carried.

As the Commander crept closer, watching these men scrabbling through the debris of the palace, he became so occupied he did not see the Earthling soldiers appear from behind the ruins of an outer wall, but as their eyes met, the Commander geared himself ready to attack. He understood the rigid mindset of fighters such as these. They accepted commands easily, but seldom broke free of their orders so he was not surprised when the two soldiers did not react quickly enough. In an instant, he shot out a powerful blast of energy that crippled their frequency, watching with satisfaction as they collapsed to the ground. Unconcerned and with hardly a glance at the unconscious men, he turned his attention back to the other humans.

He knew who he was—a soldier, a fighter, a man who acted swiftly without any care for his enemy—and for a long while he had known that this was the difference between his actions and the law Princess Chaldee stood by. Indeed, this was why he had been banished. Thoughtfully he watched the main group of soldiers. It appeared as if they were very carefully turning over what little was left of the palace. His face hardened as he remembered that terrible day. He had been held prisoner due to his role in the uprising, but as the palace came under attack Princess Chaldee had put a guard in charge of him, allowing them to move away from the prison just before the devastation began. The young guard had been so horrified by what was happening that the Commander found escape easy. For many months he had explored the new lands beyond the valley, quite overcome by the heat but staying away, afraid of what waited for him here. Then when he was unable to bear the foreign landscape another day, the Commander decided to return and try to make peace with Princess Chaldee. He felt almost grateful for the cool comfort of the valley, but he had only been here a few days when these machines reappeared.

He was still watching with puzzled concern when suddenly he found he was facing another soldier. This time it was too late. The Earthling had raised his weapon and instantly the Commander's world turned to roaring blackness. Unable to comprehend what had just happened, he collapsed into the soot and broken pieces of his lost kingdom. For a moment he lay paralyzed. The pain in his side was terrible, and he wondered how such a strange weapon could cause this agony. Barely conscious, the Commander heard the soldier speaking, but could not understand the words, then a few minutes later he felt himself being half dragged toward one of the mechanical monsters. He knew his awareness was rising and falling, for at one moment he was lying motionless trying to calm the pain, then suddenly his whole world was moving upward with a tremendous roar.

Deputy Secretary Robert McCloud stood staring down at the hospital bed, looking into the face of the man the army was claiming was one of that strange woman's compatriots. McCloud was one of the few people who had come face to face with the female they called Princess Chaldee; he knew her powers, so as he looked down at this elderly man seeming so frail in his hospital gown, he knew not to be fooled. There were only a few people who had experienced the agony caused by the mental energy these people possessed. As he was one of them, his expertise was being called upon. The trouble was, he had little comprehension of what or who the army was dealing with. These creatures seemed so alien, with mental abilities beyond anything the government, the foreign office, or even the army's Special Forces could deal with, so as he stood looking at the man in the hospital bed, Robert McCloud was amazed that they had captured him.

McCloud turned to the doctor standing beside him. "Is his physiology the same as ours?"

The doctor seemed a little amused by the question. "Naturally. Everything is where it should be."

McCloud shrugged, not wanting to take the question any further. "So, when will he regain consciousness?"

"I have no idea what you people are doing or why, but we have been instructed to keep him sedated."

"Right … good … good," McCloud said with relief. "Before he wakes you need to cover his face, or at least blindfold him. These people seem to use their eyes in some diabolical way."

The doctor did not reply, and McCloud realized that the man was completely puzzled by this demand for secrecy and also the odd behavior of anybody who came near this patient, but McCloud knew this was how it must be; they could not risk any type of attack from this strange old man.

"His wound is recovering well, so we cannot keep him like this for much longer." The doctor's tone was insistent.

"You will get instructions," McCloud said harshly. "I'm the deputy secretary of the army and I tell you it is important that you keep this man incapacitated."

"If you say so," the doctor agreed, trying to hide a smirk, which McCloud saw but decided to ignore.

The Commander had been awake and alert for at least five minutes, but he had remained motionless, so those gathered around his bed were unaware that he had regained consciousness. The vehement anger he felt as he realized that they were treating him like a dangerous animal almost blinded him to his hidden advantage. They had no idea of his skills, his ability to read the energy in the room or enter the mind of his prey, so he became calm, searching for ideas that would give him the upper hand. The people around him were unaware that he was monitoring their thoughts and although he was not sure who they were, he knew they were human and that they were afraid of him, which was pleasing. He smiled inwardly knowing he was still in control even though they had covered his eyes and strapped his arms to the bed.

"Are you awake?" McCloud moved forward, speaking softly as he tried to hide his anxiety.

"Try not to overtax this man," the nurse ordered. "He is still quite ill."

The Commander decided to acknowledge that he was awake and as he did, he began to search Robert McCloud's mind. "I'd feel better if you removed these bonds," he growled.

"We need to know who you are."

"I am the Commander of the palace guards."

"Are you a part of that woman's entourage?"

The Commander lay still, not answering, monitoring the reason behind the question. It was not difficult to learn that Chaldee had crossed paths with this silly man. It appeared that he was frightened, and that pleased the Commander; indeed, McCloud had every reason to feel afraid.

"Do you know her … this woman?"

"I have nothing to do with Princess Chaldee."

"But you are the same … ah … the same type?" McCloud asked tentatively.

The Commander renewed his assessment of the others in the room, not bothering with an answer. It seemed the man they called a doctor was not nearly as afraid as the one they called the deputy secretary. Indeed, the healing man seemed rather skeptical. There were also two women hovering near the door of the room. They, too, seemed to be involved with his health, but he could feel their anxiety, so the Commander decided to address the healer. "I am quite harmless. I beg you to untie me." As he spoke, the Commander monitored the indecision in the room. The women did not want to touch him and the human who knew of Chaldee's powers was also fearful, but the man who seemed to be able to heal was agreeable.

"I promise I will not attack any of you," the Commander begged softly. He could feel the fear and indecision from the one called McCloud, who was strongly objecting as the healer moved closer to the bed.

"Are you in pain?" the doctor asked automatically.

The Commander shook his head. "Just this restriction around my eyes."

"Leave it! We cannot afford to take off the blindfold," McCloud yelled.

"Don't be a fool, man," the doctor snapped as he pulled away the covering and stared directly into the electric blue of the Commander's eyes.

"He has already brought two soldiers down!" McCloud had backed away and was now standing with the nurses near the door.

"Thank you," the Commander said, smiling up at the doctor. "You see … I am harmless."

"You're a danger to everybody in this hospital," McCloud snarled, staring hard at the Commander before hurriedly leaving the room.

The nurses followed and the doctor grinned down at the Commander. "I am not sure what you are supposed to have done, but really I am more concerned with your wound, which I'm pleased to say is healing nicely."

"Somebody shot me," the Commander whispered in his most pathetic voice, all the time monitoring the healer's thoughts.

"I have no idea what is going on, but you are doing very well and should be able to get out of bed by tomorrow." The doctor began to remove the leather straps.

"Thank you," the Commander said as he read the other's thoughts. The healer seemed unconcerned and was preparing to leave. "Can I sit up?"

The doctor shook his head. "Not yet."

Already this man's thoughts were focused on another patient, so the Commander lay still, waiting until the room was empty before tentatively wriggling to the side of the bed, gingerly testing his ability to stand. The pain in his side and back was so severe he knew that the doctor was right. It was too soon to move, so he lay back staring around at the technical equipment. These humans might be undeveloped in some ways, but they certainly had created some amazing machines.

As soon as Robert McCloud left the Commander's hospital ward, he reached for his phone, knowing this matter was very urgent yet not sure of who to contact. Lieutenant Colonel Roccia had been transferred; anyway, he was the idiot who had caused so much trouble at that eminent, international gathering. The alien woman and her offsiders had tried to interrupt the meeting and Lieutenant Colonel Roccia was so enraged he caused a social upheaval by ordering troops to shut down the TV station—so Roccia was banished and could not be of any use. The only other person who understood what capturing the Commander meant was Skip Warner, an old friend and a highly ranked officer in the federal police. The problem was that talking to Skip about internal matters such as these might be going against government policy for although it was a matter of national security it was not part of Skip's portfolio. He rubbed the edge of the phone along his chin, trying to decide. If he called Skip at home, making it personal, between friends, it might give him an escape route if the disclosure ever became public.

Robert McCloud walked slowly to his car, pondering the ramifications, then making a sudden decision he called Skip at home. A social call would protect him, and he could casually introduce the capture of this so-called

Commander.

Skip was home nursing a twisted ankle from a skiing accident that was refusing to heal. McCloud knew about the foot but did not realize Skip had not recovered. "I'm sorry about your ankle, mate. I thought you'd be well on the mend by now."

"Well, I'm still stuck here," Skip complained.

"I don't suppose you've heard who we have in hospital."

"Yeah, yeah … I'm keeping up … even if I am a part cripple."

"Well … I've just been to see him, and … and … well … I think we are dealing with something dangerous, Skip. An army reconnaissance team working in the Kimberley said he attacked two of their men before they had a chance to react."

"McCloud," Skip warned, "I don't think we should be discussing this."

"I know, but someone needs to listen to me … this alien creature has powers we don't understand."

"Hmmm … maybe."

Skip was so noncommittal that Robert McCloud was suddenly on alert. There was something here the other man was not sharing.

"Let me rephrase that. He has powers I don't understand, but maybe you guys do?"

"Look, mate, I really can't discuss it. Sorry." Skip paused, then added offhand, "It's been a while since we had a catch-up, Bob, maybe we could meet for lunch tomorrow … you know … down at the old place."

Robert McCloud found it difficult to hide his surprise. Obviously, Skip was being very cautious, but why? Was his phone being bugged? McCloud paused for what he felt was the right length of time then causally asked: "I thought you were bedridden?"

"No … lots of damn shuffling and hobbling will get

me there."

"Well ... great!" McCloud spoke with what he hoped was the right casual emphasis. "I might have to juggle a few appointments but that's okay. Are you sure you can manage?"

"Crutches help," Skip laughed. "See you round twelve-thirty."

More than a little intrigued, Deputy Secretary Robert McCloud started his car. Maybe he was jumping to conclusions, but he had the feeling that Skip Warner might have information too secret to talk about on a phone.

Skip was already seated when Robert McCloud arrived at the café. In days passed when they were still at university, a group of friends would often come down here to the Rocks. It was the oldest part of Sydney, quiet and away from prying eyes, perfect for the conversation Robert hoped they might have today.

After they had ordered, Skip sat back in his chair, staring wordlessly across the table.

"Let's not mess around with this, Skip. If you know something, then I need to know, too. I have already crossed swords with these people—believe me, they have extraordinary powers, or their leader does, so I guess this guy in the hospital does, too. He knocked out two of our men the other day."

"Yes, we know," Skip said sharply. "We've been watching you and Roccia ever since you got back from Broken Hill. What a shambles he made of it all ... no wonder they sent him up north!"

"Ah ... is that where the idiot is now?" McCloud muttered.

"Bob, we have been working hard on this problem, so I know what you mean when you say they are dangerous. That documentary Jimmy White put to air tells us a lot about the facility up there in the Kimberley." Skip paused, then said carefully, "We think they use some type of paranormal ability … like ESP."

McCloud frowned. "Really?"

"We're a bit doubtful, but that old Commander bloke has some sort of metaphysical ability … not sure what though. We're considering interrogating Jimmy White … find out if he knows anything."

"I know White. He's in parliament now," McCloud said thoughtfully.

"An independent senator, I believe."

McCloud nodded. "You might get something out of him." He paused then added noncommittally, "But we're here now, so tell me what you know."

"Sorry, mate, can't give you all of it, but there are psychological techniques that may sort out what these people can do."

"What do you mean … techniques?"

Skip scowled. "The US military developed a type of mental monitoring system."

"Not brainwashing?" Anxiously, McCloud pushed back his chair.

"No, no! Nothing like that. We just want to understand their methods."

"What then?" McCloud said dubiously, for he had seen the type of magic the woman they called "princess" was capable of. "Have you discovered some type of secret paranormal formula?"

Skip frowned in annoyance. "No. We just want to study this guy, find out how he operates, how his mind works. He's the most valuable asset we have right now."

"Right … I see! You mean you're planning some type of examination?"

"Yes. It's why I wanted to see you today. To pick your brain … see what you can tell us."

"Hey! I don't know how those people operate," McCloud protested. "The Commander uses his eyes somehow, that's all I know."

"What about using his mind to actually control someone … maybe force them to act against their will … maybe hurt them?"

McCloud shook his head. "I don't know."

"What about remote viewing and mind reading?"

"Ah, yes … I think so … but …"

"What about telekinesis?" Skip queried excitedly, cutting across McCloud's reply.

Greatly confused, Robert McCloud shook his head.

"There's a great deal to learn here, Bob, a great deal, and we are hoping your man in hospital will give us some answers."

Robert McCloud stared across at his friend, lost in thought. He had intended to pick Skip's brain today, but instead he was being crowded with questions he could not answer, so he was relieved when their meals arrived.

Chapter Three
Chaldee's Dilemma

Chaldee sat through the meeting trying to deal with the dilemma her people were facing. While she was disappointed, in her deeper awareness she had known Joe would be unable to convince them to move into his world. She sighed aloud, and Enka, who was explaining how his people would shrivel up in such searing heat, immediately stopped speaking, bowing toward Chaldee, waiting for her to address them.

"I am sorry, Enka, my mind wandered." She paused, wondering if he had picked up her thoughts.

"What is it, Chaldee?" Paul asked with concern.

"I am finding it hard to respond." Chaldee shrugged helplessly. "For I cannot fully understand what is hidden within our present circumstances." Chaldee stopped speaking, looking around at the frowning faces, knowing such a show of uncertainty was unsettling. "You see, as well as the problems Joe and Enka are relaying, I have also been contacted by Deucallus."

"He is an important leader from another of our communities … hidden in the Andes," the Master Speaker cut in quickly trying to give Chaldee support. "But he is presently in England, helping Adele introduce her film."

"Yeah … yeah … I know who Deucallus is." Paul sounded irritated.

"From what Deucallus is reporting, the same power structure that has been interfering with us has been working against them also. He says things are becoming quite nasty in England."

"Jeez!" Worriedly, Paul ran a hand through his hair. "I don't think Jake or Adele realize exactly what we are dealing with. I reckon this interference is coming from some sort of global organization ... I should be down in Sydney, helping."

"Do you mean the military?" Joe asked.

"Maybe ... but I think it is more likely to be some consortium with international contacts."

"Yes, Deucallus is warning us all to take care."

"Chaldee, how can I get down to Sydney?" Paul asked anxiously.

"But we need you here," Enka protested.

Chaldee looked across at Paul. She knew he had not wanted to leave Sydney but had eventually given way to her persuasion, so it was understandable that he felt such a strong concern, but Enka was right, he was needed here, too. His presence was not only important to her, but to her people. He displayed both the honor and the mental strength they needed to witness. By working alongside him, she was sure they would eventually understand and accept that not all humans were evil, and if he stayed long enough, they would come to accept him as they had Joe.

"As Enka is saying, Paul, you are also needed here," she urged pointedly.

"I agree," Joe said quickly. "You know Deucallus's abilities, Paul, you have worked closely with him. You can be sure that he will protect Adele."

Paul shrugged. "But Adele is so naïve. She hasn't any idea of this danger."

"I agree, she is a sweet child." Chaldee smiled as she spoke. "But be assured, she will not come to any harm."

"Yeah ... but it's Jake who really needs me," Paul

said simply.

Chaldee nodded. "This is true, but my need is also great." She watched him carefully, hoping that he would realize the important implication of her words. Her people had always thought that the Earthlings were barbaric creatures, but she had ventured out into the human domain and had discovered this was not so; Earthlings were complicated. They were cruel, yet they were loving. They were clumsy and mindless, yet their creative skills were almost beyond comprehension.

In the cave's hazy light Chaldee cast her mind into the upper regions of consciousness, searching for the quiet voice that so often spoke to her. Right now, she needed to draw Paul into this same vastness, but he had shown little aptitude for the more profound aspects of the world he was now entering. She was beginning to understand the importance of her people's ancient prophesies, and Paul was indeed a part of the new future the Ancients had forecast. Bonds were forming between the two races, and these ties were of far-reaching importance. How could she explain to Paul that he was part of this ancient forecast?

"On the other hand," Joe was saying thoughtfully, "we really do need to pay attention to why this is happening. Why are they going to such great length to shut us down, Paul?"

"Perhaps it is to do with the powder that the professor created. It obviously has qualities that they do not want us to possess," Enka chimed in. "The professor knew this; surely it was why you helped him escape ... and why he found sanctuary here."

"Exactly ... but I have some idea of who we are dealing with ... that's why I'm concerned. I'm not sure if Jake realizes the danger," Paul said, wearily rubbing his hand across his face.

People sat listening, nodding in sympathy.

"Madame, it would seem that we are facing

tremendous difficulties," the Master Speaker said sadly. "Our direction is not clear, and our involvement with the Earthlings is becoming more and more perplexing, very little of which can be found in the Ancients' prophesies."

Chaldee listened to her main advisor, not wanting to explain the importance of combining the two races. She knew the scrolls had ended with the reuniting of the two worlds. Their position now, as they searched for a new home and were forced to confront the power of the Earthlings, was absent from any prediction, but she allowed her mind to sink deeper, to where their future held the promise of something very new. "I believe that we are like pioneers, journeying into the wilderness." She paused and looked around at the questioning faces. "We are being forced to step into the future, to take a new direction. This is a time of great upheaval. The planet is speaking, and people everywhere need to seek a new direction. Now that we have found we can unite with the Earthling race it gives us a chance to begin a heartfelt exchange that has not been present in our civilization for thousands of years. Everybody, I think this is the beginning of an extraordinary communion with our two races."

"And we need courage," the Master Speaker said quietly.

"We need persistence, too." Joe stood up as he spoke. "Chaldee, I agree with you. I believe this is a critical time, and Paul is right when he suggests we should search deeper into this cave system. We might solve our problems if we try to find what is hidden in the deeper reaches of the Earth, search there for what might be waiting for us."

As Joe spoke, Chaldee shivered with excitement. She felt there was profound meaning in his words, but the fullness of what was being hinted had not yet touched her core. She glanced around at the group and then back to Paul.

"Yes … well … I've read about a cave in Vietnam," Paul said carefully. "It's so huge, so different from anything we understand that it creates its own weather system, even its own clouds!"

"I know … you told me about it … maybe exploring these caves is something we might try," Joe suggested quietly.

Paul seemed pleased by Joe's support. "Well, maybe there is something like that here, too. We don't know much about the inner Earth. The Son Doong cave is so large it dwarfs everything that is known. If we could find something similar, it might be our answer!"

Chaldee listened, still feeling a tingle of excitement, but it was mixed with fear for she knew what Paul was proposing was overflowing with unknown dangers. "I see you and Joe are determined to investigate, and I am sure there is something waiting to be found, although I suspect you will face a few difficulties on the way." Chaldee turned to Master Zell. "What do you think, Master Speaker? Should they try?"

The Master Speaker seemed to ponder the question as he gazed across at Paul. "Perhaps, Madame! If the caves could give us a way forward, it might be the new direction you speak about."

Suddenly excited, Paul stood up. "Okay, Joe," he said loudly, slapping Joe on the back. "Do you reckon we could give it a go?"

Chaldee realized that everybody at the meeting could feel Paul's excitement and this gave them new hope. "We must plan this expedition carefully," she said, smiling at Paul's sudden enthusiasm, pleased that he had pushed aside his worry about Jake and Adele. She was not concerned for them, but she could not help fearing what might be awaiting Paul in the dark reaches of the hollow Earth.

"We need to gather supplies," Enka said quietly,

"plan for every situation."

"We need climbing and diving gear, food, lights, digging tools, protective clothing." Paul was methodically listing their needs on his fingers.

"Who will go with you?" the Master Speaker asked.

"I think three of us to start with. Both Joe and Enka are really capable. We'll venture in just a little way … get a feel for exactly what's there."

Joe nodded. "Yeah … right … let's plan to spend twenty-four hours in there. That way you will know when to expect us back. Enka can telepathically keep in touch with Princess Chaldee, so there should not be any risk."

"I will reflect on all possibilities, for we must be sure that we do not cause any further complications," Chaldee said softly. "I will meditate. This will give us the guidance we need."

The meeting broke up. Paul, Joe, and Enka had help as they began to gather what they would need, others set about their daily tasks, and Chaldee withdrew into the small but majestic enclosure they had built for her. Here in the soft half-light, she reached out to the unseen assistance that had so often helped her. Ascending into the uppermost reaches of consciousness, Chaldee's meditation lifted her into other realms and she began to search for the help Paul would need.

Chaldee organized the cave's working group, the people who maintained the day-to-day running of the cave, and they helped Paul and Joe gather the gear needed for this venture. At the end of a tiring afternoon most of their equipment was piled up in the end cave. This area was very low and dark, but there was a narrow slit leading into a damp passageway. It was an area Paul had already ventured into; in fact, it was why he felt so certain there was something farther in worth looking at. They would leave in the morning and planned to be away no more than twenty-four hours.

Chaldee could not help noticing that their enthusiasm had created a buzz of excitement around the cave. The mere suggestion of a way forward seemed to have fired up hope.

The day was slipping into evening and Chaldee saw Paul wander outside. She found him perched on the rocks overlooking the valley and immediately she could feel his tension. He certainly was not sharing Joe and Enka's excitement.

"I know you want to go back to your city, to Jake, to be of some help, but we need you here, too … you must know that."

"It's more than that, Chaldee; it's also a question of our relationship—you and me; it's how stupid I often feel around you." Paul was struggling to find the right words. "So … so … should I be here with you? I mean … with all the troubles facing Jake and Adele, maybe I should be with them."

"Please, Paul," she whispered. "We need patience. Insight. I know this is a difficult time, but please, try to think ahead. Move past these difficult circumstances."

Paul nodded miserably. "I'm not sure what is happening with us, Chaldee. I know your position here takes up much of your time and you must give them direction, but …"

"I am sorry." Chaldee spoke softly as she tentatively touched his face. She realized how uncertain he felt as he tried to adjust to this new life. Their realities were challenging, yet she knew he loved her. "Paul, it's vital that we approach these differences with great care." Chaldee took his hands, raising them to her lips. "If you care, as you say you do, then please give me your trust. My feelings have not changed, but as you say, my position here takes much of my attention."

Paul turned away helplessly. "I know, Chaldee, I know. It's just hard to accept, when your place here is so …" He paused then muttered, "So damn regal!"

"What you really mean, Paul, is that my position here is causing you discomfort."

Paul wrapped his arms around her. "I did not realize just how rigid I am," he whispered apologetically. "It's hard to take a step back … you know I often feel absolutely useless here! In a way I think that's why I want to get back to Jake … back to what I know … to being of some use."

Chaldee shook her head, dismayed, but fully aware of his confusion. Here was somebody who had always taken the lead in decision making. Paul was the one who offered solutions, who helped solve problems, but now he was being forced to stay in the background and abide by her rules. "I am sorry," she repeated sadly.

They stood together in a sad embrace, both feeling the strain. At last Chaldee stepped back, touching his face gently. "These differences will eventually be accepted … by both of us. What you have to offer here is vast. Your pragmatic approach to problems and your honesty has such a noble quality; they are priceless assets, Paul. Your intention to explore the caves for our benefit, these actions are being noticed by everyone." She reached up and kissed him warmly. "Your presence here is vital."

Chaldee was aware that he was still feeling wretchedly confused, so as a ploy she decided to change the subject and share another problem. "Paul, I think maybe you could help shed light on another of our differences. You are aware of the man the Earthling soldiers took away, the Commander."

Paul frowned, looking uncertain. "The guy they shot?"

Chaldee nodded. "He was an outcast for he had acted against all the principles of our race, but I never wished this to happen to him, to be wounded and taken away by those Earthling soldiers."

"It's a bad scene, I agree."

Because she had captured Paul's interest, Chaldee knew she must choose her words carefully. "The Commander has skills almost equal to my own, so his capture will be treated as a victory by some of your people. Although he was my enemy I do not like what is happening to him. He has mentally contacted me telling me that they are anxious to understand who he is. In his telepathic message he used the word 'mine'—they want to mine his skills!"

"Exactly. Of course, they do," Paul said contemptuously.

"But I am concerned by how they might approach this."

"It doesn't sound good … believe me, their psychological manipulations are ugly."

Instantly his words caused a shiver of horror to ripple through her. "Let's go back inside. I am feeling uncomfortable." She saw Paul's look of concern but turned away so he could not see the fear his words had caused. Paul's disdain was similar to the Commander's angry tone but although the feeling in his message had been one of scorn, he had reached out, and she realized immediately that his need was great as he telepathically shared images of his poorly lit restricted cell and the ugly blindfold they had bound around his head. He said very little, just asked that she send him extra energy if needed. She had agreed but their brief exchange was upsetting and now as she began to explain the situation, her anxiety grew. "I fear that they will hurt him," she whispered as they moved back into the cave.

"They'll try to take him apart, Chaldee. He has the

type of mental powers they have been messing around with for years. They can already reshape a victim's mind. It's ugly … so your man needs to get out of there somehow."

Chaldee felt angry, for although Paul's words caused more fear, she was also outraged as she understood his warning. Humans were so cruel when they were fighting each other or seeking personal power. These were the traits that disgusted her people; it was why they loathed the Earthlings.

"What's wrong?" Joe asked as he joined them.

"Very often these days I feel as if I have lost all ability to make decisions." Chaldee was shaking her head as she spoke.

Paul's glance was grim. "Hi, Joe. Chaldee is facing the threat we have been dealing with for years!"

"Yes … but there are other things one can do," Joe suggested quietly. "By waiting and reflecting on a problem one can often find a way through."

Chaldee looked at Joe, feeling a sense of relief as she heard his words. "You are right. This is exactly what we need to do—we must bide our time."

"Meanwhile, we have collected most of what we need for tomorrow," Joe changed the subject. "Maybe we could have a small farewell party after our meal tonight."

"Of course!" Chaldee beamed a huge smile, spontaneously hugging Joe as she realized what he was asking. Everyone would want to wish them well, and such a happy gathering was exactly what was needed.

Joe grinned at Paul. "Cheer up, mate, things could be much worse."

Chaldee watched as they began to examine the right equipment, then her mind returned to the troubles the Commander was facing. There was much she needed to explore. The Commander was beginning to deal with the dark forces that Paul was very aware of, so it would seem she needed to be open to the stream of information that was always available.

As Chaldee made her way back to her private quarters, she pondered over Joe's advice. She had long been aware of the huge changes happening both here and in the world of the Earthlings; now, as Joe said, she must reflect, examine, and try to gauge her people's future. Gently closing the entrance so everybody would know not to disturb her, Chaldee began to drift into a deep meditation. At first her mind remained occupied by the Commander's disturbing message, but gradually she was taken far beyond all physical reality, past the restriction of time, to a place where all information was ratified by Truth. Saturated by this energy Chaldee remained in the stillness for some time, then slowly as she again became aware, she began to experience what felt like a massive upheaval of the planet. Shocked, her mind immediately went to the cave area that Paul wanted to explore, but this felt different. It seemed to be beneath the water, a massive under-ocean earthquake. As she let herself flow into the premonition, she could feel the might of this shifting, thrusting movement. Then suddenly Earth seemed to erupt out of the ocean. The image was gone as quickly as it had filled her mind, leaving her with a helpless feeling that was so unusual it snapped her awake. Greatly puzzled, she pondered over what she had just witnessed. It was obviously some type of earthquake, or maybe the beginnings of a volcanic eruption; whatever it was, it was huge, and it was serious.

Almost in a panic, Chaldee hurried out into the main cave, calling for Zell.

"Your Highness," the Master Speaker bowed his head.

"A few moments ago, in my reverie, I seemed to sense some type of imminent upheaval in the vastness of the ocean."

The Master Speaker frowned. "An upheaval,

Madame?"

"I am quite amazed, Zell." Chaldee paused, trying to find a way of describing her vision without causing alarm.

"You foresaw such a thing, Madame?"

"Not here, Zell. Somewhere out there," she said, waving vaguely toward the east. "It would seem that there might be a rising up of new land, or maybe an earthquake under the ocean. I am not really sure."

"It seems to have left a strong impression, Your Highness."

"It was enormous, Zell, enormous. Even the image exhausted me."

The Master Speaker was silent. Chaldee knew her vision was worrying him, but she had been given a warning that she knew she must share.

"Whatever is ahead, I don't think we are in danger—yet. It felt to be farther to the east, beyond what the Earthlings call their mainland."

"This warning must be of great importance, Madame. Perhaps others have also had the premonition."

Chaldee nodded. "You are right, Zell, but yet I feel I must reach out, let the human authorities know what is ahead."

"Did it feel to be imminent?"

"It did, Zell, as if the catastrophe is about to occur. As I say, I do not think we are in danger here, but during my meditation the images I became aware of were very disturbing. I think perhaps their entire eastern coastline might be under threat if there is a tsunami."

"Whom should we tell, Madame? How can we inform them?"

Chaldee shook her head at the distasteful idea that had suddenly occurred. "Zell, as yet I have not told you, but the Commander has made contact."

"Oh no!"

Chaldee nodded. "He has been captured and the

Earthling authorities want him to spy for them."

"Madame, this is impossible!"

"It is certainly a strange situation. I have advised against it, but of course the Commander will act as he will act, Zell. We have never had control of that man." Her smile was grim. "Nevertheless, I am thinking that he is the one I should inform of my vision."

"This is such an outlandish situation, Your Highness. To think we must engage the Commander in such a way. It's outrageous, for that man is truly our enemy."

"I know," Chaldee said, nodding slowly as she considered the idea. "But he is the only one who can receive such a dire warning. There will be a tidal wave which will devastate the land, and the Earthlings need to be warned."

"But the Commander," Zell complained. "Do you feel you must reach out?"

"I do." Chaldee took a deep breath. "There is no other solution, Zell."

They stared at each other, trying to comprehend this blatant twist of destiny, forcing Chaldee to engage with someone the entire community regarded as an enemy. Eventually she turned inward and once again made contact with the Commander.

Chapter Four
The Commander Gains Control

In a well-hidden facility close to Sydney University, where the "Law" held captive those they considered people of interest, the Commander was trying to remain calm. He was still blindfolded and the two officers attempting to force him along the passageway were unaware that he was monitoring their thoughts. His resistance was automatic for he had never been treated like this before; nevertheless, even as he fought back, he was assessing what they were thinking. Amid the curses and the struggling he realized that he was about to be interviewed by an authority neither of these men approved of.

The room they were pushing him into was bright, so obviously there must be windows, perhaps even sunlight. The Commander was amazed at how it affected him for he had not realized how much he needed to feel the sun.

"Take off the blindfold," a male voice ordered.

The Commander heard the contemptuous authority in this voice, and as he monitored this new thought pattern, he realized he was in the presence of what the Earthlings called a clinical psychologist, but why would somebody like this take on the role of an investigator?

The covering was lifted and with great relief the

Commander could see the space around him. He was in a large room, sun lit and very comfortable, and he could not help but be impressed by the huge windows, the high ceiling, but even more satisfying was the energy he felt as the sunlight filtered into the room. Quietly the Commander began to observe his interrogator, monitoring his thoughts and calculating each nuance of meaning. It seemed that the man on the other side of the table was not worried by any threat this unbinding might pose and as he continued to mind-read, the Commander realized they were about to offer him some type of reward.

"Sit."

The Commander obeyed, watching carefully. The two jailers who had brought him into this room were now standing by the door and both were holding those small human weapons.

"Attack me and they will shoot," the investigator said coldly.

The Commander shrugged but said nothing.

"So, I am here to assess your abilities and to talk a little about what we can offer you."

The Commander nodded slowly, still reading the other's mind, and quite surprised by this approach. For at least two days he had been locked in the dark, deliberately kept cold and uncomfortable with only water to drink; now suddenly it had all been reversed. Another tactic perhaps?

"We are very interested in the mental skills you displayed when you attacked the soldiers."

"I should imagine they have regained their senses by now," the Commander said evenly as he stared intensely into his inquisitor's eyes. Immediately the man began to tremble, so the Commander quickly averted his gaze, smiling as he read the fury in the other's mind. This man was angry at being made a victim so easily. Suddenly enjoying himself, the Commander turned to the guard. "I think you missed that," he sniggered.

In the heavy, sullen silence that followed, the Commander could feel his opponent's air of domination beginning to fade. Desperately the investigator was attempting to regain control. It satisfied the Commander as he realized the man was shocked at how easily he had been overpowered.

Eventually the psychologist seemed stable enough to continue, but his authority was gone. "Tell me how you use your energy. You seem to project it in some way?"

The Commander sat motionless, aware that he was in control, but wise enough to appear to be the victim.

"Have you any idea of what you are doing or how you actually do it?" the psychological profiler asked grimly.

"The energy system of my people differs greatly from your Earthling race." As he spoke, the Commander could see the confusion, almost fear that his words evoked. This man did not feel safe now it had been established that he was in the room with an alien being. "We use our energy to heal, but if we are in danger, we use it to disable."

"But how?" The man opposite had dropped all pretense of control and was leaning forward. "Can you explain how this is done?"

"I believe you people use something similar, but from what I have heard, you must almost destroy the victim's mind first. Your programs of control take a great deal of time and personnel."

The investigator's lips tightened. "No … we don't use such methods in this country."

"But you are aware of them, of how barbaric they are!"

"You obviously use a different form of control." The man across the desk tried to relax but his ongoing agitation caused the Commander to smile, delighted by how the interview was going. He turned to look at the guards at the door, noting that they were so interested in the conversation they had lowered their weapons. Aware of the change in atmosphere, the Commander realized he could probably walk away at any time, but as he continued to mind-read he saw there was an opportunity here. They could use his skills, they wanted him, and this meant they were giving him a priceless bargaining tool, so he shifted slightly in his chair but said nothing.

"Have you any way of explaining your skills?"

"We interfere with the body's electrical system," the Commander said quietly. "You Earthlings call this field around your body an aura; we have the ability to interrupt the flow."

"How? What do you use?"

"Our energy," the Commander said with disdain.

"Are you aware … or does this happen automatically?"

"I repeat that our race is different from your own. We vibrate at a different frequency, our density is less, and we are not as influenced by the Earth's energy as you people are."

"So, when you attack our consciousness, what are you doing?" the investigating officer asked with a persistency that was beginning to annoy the Commander.

"We do not attack; we smother your body flow. We can also influence your mind."

"You can read my mind … are you reading me now?" The psychologist was so shocked that the Commander had to pull his attention away, amazed by the sudden mental chaos he was feeling. This man was not stable.

"You are interfering with me!" The last words were high pitched as the investigator reeled back. One guard rushed across to help as the man fell across the desk.

"Give him some water," the Commander ordered. "And undo that jacket thing he's wearing."

The guard obeyed, and slowly the distraught man regained control. The Commander sat inert and indifferent.

He had already accepted that they needed his skill, so now he had to wait until the real authority arrived. This man was obviously just a messenger.

Within an hour of the psychologist's collapse, the Commander was brought back to the same large, well-lit room, but now the desk had been pushed against the wall and there was a couch and a few comfortable chairs.

"Please sit."

The Commander found a chair and looked across at the two men who seemed quite relaxed and comfortable. They were not trying to shield their thoughts from him. He realized that he had seen one of the men before, but his memory was vague.

"I'm Robert McCloud, deputy secretary of the army. I visited you in hospital and this is my associate Skip Warner."

The Commander stared quizzically at the two Earthlings. "And?"

"Your little performance before was quite surprising," McCloud said, nodding toward the camera high in the corner of the room. "We watched with interest."

The Commander was silent.

"Of course, we understand that you feel … ah … under threat here, but really this is wrong. We do not wish you any harm."

"No," Skip cut in quickly. "Really, we are intrigued by your skills."

"Indeed, we would like to work with you," McCloud said probingly, his words sounding rather like a question.

The Commander heard this as a plea, and as he read the thoughts of both men, he realized that they had an actual task in mind.

"But we understand that you may be missing your home … your people," Skip said pleasantly. "And you can return there, at any time … we are not keeping you prisoner."

"No, not at all," McCloud agreed.

Both men were waiting so the Commander stood up and walked over to the window. "I am not sure if I can be here for very long. Your system is not really to my liking," he said slowly as he gazed down into the street. "Your machinery is ugly and very loud, and from the little I have seen, your people seem on the brink of some type of nervous madness." He turned back to them. "I can feel it swelling up from down there. Some are almost mindless, aren't they?" The Commander watched as McCloud took a deep breath, and as he read the other's mind the Commander realized that McCloud was remembering how Chaldee had made almost the same accusation when she had attacked them at the Broken Hill mine.

"We understand that your culture must be different but hear us out," Skip said quickly as if trying to shield McCloud. "If you would sit down, we have a proposal to put forward."

The Commander remained at the window, tugging at the strange pants given to him at the hospital. They felt tight and itchy. "Well, right now I'm only interested in these clothes. They are too tight, and they scratch my skin … why is everything here so restrictive?" The Commander took off his sandals and wandered back to his chair. "This constraint is very limiting, almost like an obstacle to growth." He stared across at McCloud. "You Earthlings seem to suffer some type of bondage."

The Commander could see that Robert McCloud was finding it difficult to hold his temper so in contempt he waggled a warning finger. "Be calm, sir, and let us talk about what you are proposing. It would seem you want me to monitor a man who has been causing problems for your organization. Yes?" As neither man answered, the Commander continued. "Then I need to fully understand what and who he is, and why you want this … so define the details please."

Skip Warner glanced despairingly first at McCloud and then at the Commander. "Well … ah … yes. You are right, this is what we are hoping for. This man has connections to people who are hiding vital material that belongs to the state."

"Highly experimental research," McCloud added.

The Commander frowned. "But I see you are a little unsure about this material … you are calling it a powder … so what is it? What does it do? Why this urgency to get it back?" The Commander paused as he continued to read Skip's mind. "Ah … I see … this amazing material is not yours, is it?"

McCloud shrugged. "The discovery is too important to be in the hands of civilians."

The Commander's stare was probing and intense. "What are we really dealing with here? What are you asking of me?"

"This is an extremely dangerous situation. These people intend to distribute this material without having any idea of its potential."

"And are these people connected to me?" The Commander paused as he probed McCloud's mind. "Oh! I see … they are friends of Princess Chaldee."

"Yes," Skip said simply.

The Commander leaned forward, staring first at Robert McCloud then at Skip Warner. "Now I think we can talk. Now I am beginning to understand."

"Are you saying you are interested?" Skip said, suddenly fired with enthusiasm.

"Indeed."

"So maybe you could stay here in Sydney for a little

while … just as a trial, of course."

"Perhaps juggle your life so you could live both here and in your own culture. You would be well compensated if you decided to work for us," Robert McCloud added.

"I do not work for any person," the Commander snapped. "But I am intrigued by what you believe I can do and where I can live."

Skip nodded with enthusiasm. "Your abilities are far greater than ours, so your input would be tremendous. You are …"

"I want to live in a large space like this," the Commander insisted, rudely cutting across Skip's excitement.

"Of course."

"And return to my home whenever I choose."

Again, both men nodded, although the Commander saw a cloud of doubt ripple through McCloud's mind. "I see you will need to convince others of what I demand."

"Not everyone in our organization knows about you or the skillset you offer, but as they learn more, they won't object."

The Commander nodded unconcerned, then leaning back in his chair he muttered, "I like this furniture, it offers great comfort."

"If you agree then we will find you a place today, somewhere like this, a place you can enjoy," McCloud said eagerly.

"And we can start your training as soon as you feel ready," Skip added.

"I am pleased," the Commander said autocratically as he pushed farther back into his chair. "And now I shall sleep."

The two men looked at each other, both shocked and surprised, then Skip grinned. "The man commands and we obey."

The Commander could remember the few times he had felt real fear, but now, traveling in the machine they called a car, he was afraid. The speed was horrific, and the closeness of the machines around them presented the greatest threat he had ever experienced.

"We've booked you into a serviced apartment in Coogee. It will only be for a few nights … hope that's okay," Robert McCloud muttered, unaware of the Commander's state as he busily worked his phone.

The Commander clasped and unclasped his hands trying to appear calm as he watched the vehicle travel headlong toward disaster. The machine stopped when all the other machines stopped, then reared up again as the entire fleet rushed forward. He was about to demand they stop when an even more amazing sight appeared. A large expanse of blue water was spreading unhindered in front of him. So boundless, so vast, it seemed to touch the sky. "What is it?" he demanded fiercely, pointing toward the sea.

McCloud could hear the Commander's alarm. "This is what we refer to as an ocean."

"I have heard of this thing," the Commander said stiffly, "but I had no idea of its color or its size."

"Sydney is built around water. You'll get used to it," McCloud said in a casual voice, totally unaware of the Commander's shock.

They traveled the rest of the way in silence, but the Commander's mind was frantic. This world he had been thrown into was so extraordinary his whole sense of reality was being threatened, yet he was a warrior, a title that demanded courage. He must regain his spirit. He closed his eyes, trying to shut out these bizarre surroundings, and as he did so he suddenly became aware that Chaldee was reaching out to him. Shuddering, he grabbed McCloud's arm. "Stop!" Viciously, the Commander stared into Robert McCloud's face. "You must stop this machine."

As Robert McCloud felt the intensity of the Commander's gaze, he began to lose consciousness. The driver slowed to a stop, then turned to see his boss falling across the back seat.

The Commander did not hesitate; awkwardly scrambling out of the car he hurried toward what seemed to be a stand of trees scattered across a green field. Even the sight of the trees offered him some sense of calm. Breathing deeply, he slowed his pace, allowing Chaldee's thoughts to flood in. She seemed very anxious and for a moment he thought maybe she was aware of his plight, but then he realized she was giving him instructions.

Trying to clear his head, the Commander slumped onto a wooden bench under one of the trees. "Madame, I am in a difficult situation. When I have resolved the problem, I will resume contact." Closing down all communication, the Commander dropped his head in his hands, and for the first time in his long life he felt crushed, almost despairing.

He was still sitting with head in hand when the driver caught up with him. "Mate, I don't know what you did, but Mr. McCloud is not happy."

The Commander shrugged.

"He wants to see you … in the car."

"I must sit here a little longer … to re-energize."

"Sorry, fella," the driver said roughly as he took hold of the Commander's arm. "We gotta go."

The Commander stiffened. "I said I will remain here," he said firmly. "Tell your master to return in an hour."

For a moment the driver seemed undecided, then wordlessly he turned away and the Commander knew he had been given time to recuperate so he settled, feeling the vital energy of the tree he was sitting under, and after a time of stillness and relaxation he returned his attention to Chaldee. "Madame, what is your message?"

There was no answer, so the Commander lay back on the bench, and breathing deeply, he began to regain his balance. This human world was affecting him in a way he had never imagined. As an elder, he was endowed with a sense of well-being, a calmness that was now being threatened by something he did not understand, and this was causing more agitation.

Eventually Chaldee's message filtered through and he realized she was warning him about an earthquake and tsunami that were about to occur. He knew her skill in slipping between timelines, so he had no doubt that what she was forecasting was serious. "But, Madame, I do not think the authorities here will pay heed to anything I have to say."

"The earthquake is under the sea; it will be caused as new land rises. It will create a massive wave so make sure the Earthlings are prepared."

"I fully understand, and I will pass on the message, Madame, but this is all I can do." The Commander was shaking his head as he answered. He knew they would not listen.

For the next hour the Commander sat motionless under the tree, soothing his emotional state and regaining his focus. He thought about Chaldee's message, but he had no idea how he could make the humans listen. These people had no sense of a wider reality. With a frustrated sigh, the Commander again focused on his inner world so by the time Robert McCloud returned he felt self-assured and back in command.

Chapter Five
Calamity Strikes

In the main cave, Paul, Joe, and Enka were carrying out a final check of their gear. The atmosphere was tense as people gathered to watch and comment, even Joe was a little agitated, wanting to be on the move, but Chaldee was not there so they knew they must wait.

Chaldee was again deep in meditation, allowing information to flood in as she asked for guidance. She was shown the route through the cave system. It looked narrow in places, with a few small rivulets of water, but there did not seem to be any great hazard. Eventually she moved back to the present, aware that they were all waiting for her parting words, but she did not feel positive, or gracious; she was afraid for Paul, afraid he would suffer, or perhaps even die. For Chaldee these feelings were new; such terrifying fears for another person caused a strange pain, something she was not used to. She had loved her father, but had not feared for his safety, but as she had helped Paul with their preparation, she was afraid, and this was unnerving.

Eventually Chaldee made her way to the departure point, at the far end of the livable caves. It was dank and quite dark, so she wasted no time giving her blessings. The three young men said their quick good-byes and magically disappeared through the small opening that

Paul had discovered a few weeks earlier. At that time, she had ventured a little way along the narrow passageway, but the atmosphere had felt sour. The Earth seemed to fold in around her so that she could not hide from its overwhelming mass. Now as she watched them disappear, she was reminded again of the incomprehensible magnitude of the planet.

Abruptly all sound of their movement was lost. There was no hint of their presence; they were gone. With a silent whimper of despair, Chaldee led her flock back to the main cave where her Master Speaker was preparing for a special meeting; this was so everybody could combine in a collective prayer. The force of this unity of protective thought was strong, and Chaldee hoped it would help safeguard the three young men. Not one person protested, for all knew the importance of this mission. It was their only hope of finding a new home. Her people formed a series of harmonious circles around Chaldee, and quietly they began to join minds, forming strong loops of energy that grew stronger as their intention deepened. They began to see the goal that those exploring were aiming for, and as the group focused on this place, they allowed it to grow and form, using the energies of the third dimension to create a dreamy reality.

The light on Paul's headlamp spread along a rocky downward path. It was low, rough, and only wide enough for one person to pass. To Paul, it felt as if they were inside some obscure crack in the world, but after pushing, wriggling, and sometimes crawling, the passageway leveled out, widening into a high narrow cave.

The three grouped together so their lights were

strong enough to penetrate the utter blackness. It appeared that they were on a wide ledge that ran around the rim of a deep void.

"I think there's another cave down there. This place seems to have at least two levels," Joe said.

Paul nodded. "How far do you reckon the drop is?"

Both Enka and Joe leaned out farther so their lights rippled across the very jagged, uneven terrain below, the brightness catching the beauty of the flowstones, accentuating a large shawl formation of stalactites fanning across the opposite wall, then farther down along the floor of the cave there seems to be vague pillar-like shapes of stalagmites, but their lights were not powerful enough to fully reveal the ruggedness of this dark place.

"Not far … I reckon it'd be about thirty feet, give or take," Joe said as he stared down trying to penetrate the chasm's darkness. "And I think there might be water down there."

"I reckon we could abseil down …"

"Paul," Enka broke in, "see how this path continues upward, maybe we could follow it first before we try to go down."

Paul scratched his head thoughtfully. "Okay … that'll keep us on this level … but we need to keep testing our footing in case the whole thing gives way. I doubt if it's ever had to hold our weight before!"

Joe stared around suddenly overwhelmed by the wonder of this hidden world. "Yeah … you're right … nobody's ever been here before! Crickey! It's like walking on the moon!"

All three were suddenly in awe. Up until this moment, they had been occupied by the practical demands of the tunnel but the majestic yet unfathomable feel of this dark space, locked away for aeons of time came surging up, silent yet overpowering.

Eventually Paul picked up his gear, and the three

began to slowly inch forward. They were not sure where they were heading because of the hollow silence and the total blackness, but for the next few hours they pushed forward through this cavernous funnel, at times stumbling or tripping over loose rocks. This rubble had been building up over aeons of time and was quite hazardous, but they were unable to see exactly where they were, limited by the inadequacy of their lights in the vastness of this subterranean fortress. The route had become narrow, and they had been pushing hard for some time when straight ahead Paul could see a huge boulder blocking their path. "Wow … looks like a dead-end."

The three came to a hesitant stop, suddenly realizing they were hemmed in by the weight of this underground world.

"No! Look! There's a gap," Joe said optimistically. "I think we can get past." Joe took off his backpack, pushing it past the large boulder then wriggled through after it. After a moment he popped his head back through the gap. "Hey! It's much wider on this side and I think it leads down into another cave."

Wordlessly Enka followed but Paul was a larger build than the other two and as he forced his way through, he became stuck. Using his shoulder Paul gave a powerful heave, pushing hard against the rock. It still did not move, and a jolt of panic caught in his throat as he realized he was trapped. Fiercely, and now almost in panic, Paul pounded at the immovable boulder. Suddenly there was a groaning, tearing sound as the huge rock began to shudder. Paul could do nothing as the entire wall-face started to slip. Horrified, he realized the boulder and the cave wall were collapsing; debris was hurtling into the darkness and Paul, unable to gain any sort of traction, also began to fall.

Joe could see what was happening. It seemed the whole side of the cave had disintegrated. He gave a frantic yell as he made a grab for Paul, but it was pointless. His friend had already disappeared into the bruising emptiness.

For a few seconds Enka and Joe were paralyzed. The noise of the falling rock drowned Paul's cries, so they had no idea where he might be or how deep the chasm was.

Cautiously Joe moved toward the gaping hole, but Enka grabbed him. "You should lay on your stomach, Joe. I'll hold your feet."

Joe nodded, and on his stomach with Enka gripping his legs he squirmed over to the edge, but his light was too weak. "I can't see anything … just dust. I need my torch."

Enka helped him back and with trembling fingers Joe broke open his backpack, searching frantically for his large torch.

Again, he scrambled to the edge with Enka holding him safe, and now in the strength of the torchlight Joe was able to make out what he thought was Paul laying not far below them on a ledge. "I think I see him." He swung the light around the whole area but could see nothing in the dusty light. "Maybe we should use ropes to assess the fall factor before we go down there … but it doesn't seem far."

"Test the area around you. Is it strong?"

Joe pushed and banged the rock around the edge. It felt solid. "I think it's okay."

Without a word, Enka let go of Joe's legs and wriggled over beside him. Together they squinted into the blackness, assessing the area and the risk.

"All Paul's gear went over with him, so we've only got a few ropes."

"Doesn't matter, we can anchor a rope around those rocks," Joe said, pointing to a rock cluster jutting out from the cave wall. "I'll just have to loop the rope around my waist, and you can feed it out as I go down."

Wordlessly they set about making the climb safe and within ten minutes of the collapse Joe was abseiling down toward the ledge where Paul lay. Joe called out as he descended but there was no answer. Then as he edged his way onto the ledge, he saw immediately that Paul was unconscious, lying motionless on his back. He called up to Enka for another rope, but as he began to lash it around Paul's body, his friend groaned. Hesitantly Joe drew back, suddenly realizing that safety wasn't the priority here, maybe Paul's back was seriously injured. Sitting back on his heels, Joe gently began to feel under Paul's body, and again Paul groaned as he was moved. Frantically Joe called up to Enka again. "I can't move him. I think it's really bad, Enka. You'll have to get help. I'll stay here."

"I can reach out to Chaldee now, Joe. What do we need?"

Joe almost smiled. In his panic he had forgotten these people used telepathy. "Some type of stretcher maybe … I'm not sure. Tell her what's happened; she may …" But in midsentence Joe's words spluttered to a halt as he began to see the slightest flickering of what appeared to be a hazy light hovering to one side of the ledge. "Hey … what is that?" Joe's words stumbled into a puzzled silence as in the middle of the darkness, in midair, the light expanded, and to his amazement Joe could see a figure beginning to materialize. Shaking his head Joe drew back against the rock wall, too dumbstruck to feel afraid.

Then the floating figure spoke: "… and my friends, tell Princess Chaldee I am coming. I need to collect some of that magical powder."

Joe could see that the figure was now fully formed, and it seemed to be simply hovering in midair. "Who … what … are you?" he whispered, staring at this very tall, very thin figure who was surrounded by a flickering glow. It had an exceptionally large head and wonderful eyes.

The apparition smiled. "I am known as Isaak, and

I can see that your need is very urgent. Your friend is severely injured."

"But … you are … floating?"

"I have the ability to move interdimensionally, gravity being quite a trivial concern … anyway, as you can see there is no room on that ledge for a third person … so here I am." Isaak laughed cheerfully.

Joe was still aghast because he was not sure whether he was imagining the whole scene. "Did you hear anything, Enka?" he yelled, wanting somebody else to confirm this sudden, quite unreal interruption.

"I heard it, Joe, something about the professor's powder," Enka yelled, his voice filled with wonder.

Blindly Joe stared at this strange floating figure, suddenly unable to speak.

"Be calm, my friend. I am here to help."

As Isaak spoke, Joe felt a sudden flow of soothing energy, and slowly he began to relax. He did not really understand what was happening, but it seemed somehow, this person was here to help. "You say your name is Isaak?"

"Yes, and we need to hurry. I will transfer to the caves immediately … so warn your princess I am coming and that I need the powder, it will greatly help your friend."

Joe was still amazed at what appeared to be some magical apparition, but he tried to regain some sense of reality then Isaak chuckled again as he disappeared.

Joe yelled back up to Enka. "Warn Chaldee that someone is coming for the powder."

"What?"

"Just do it, Enka." Joe took a deep breath, unable to explain. "Just tell her."

Enka did not answer so Joe was hopeful that the message was getting through. Then with a feeling of relief he smiled down at his unconscious friend, intuitively understanding that in some weird way, they were being helped. Reaching out, Joe tentatively took Paul's hand, not wanting to cause any more damage, but needing to reassure him.

Chapter Six
Underground City

Although Chaldee was unaware of the accident, she had felt extremely anxious about Paul's plan, so in an effort to ignore this inner warning she busied herself with her daily duties, organizing her usual team of six who went down once a week to scrounge through what was left of their village. For months, she had been sending out groups to scour the area, searching among the wreckage, bringing back the tattered remnants of ancient writings, of history and science as well as practical items such as food, plants, furniture, sheep, goats, and anything else that they felt they needed to make life a little more comfortable in the caves. This activity had kept the overall attitude positive but since the return of the invading soldiers, she was being careful, sending smaller groups out in the late afternoon, making sure they were constantly aware of the danger.

Once her team of scavengers had departed, Chaldee turned her attention to the persistent telepathic message that had been trying to force its way into her consciousness for over an hour and knew immediately the Commander was trying to reach her again. In the days after the uprising, she had blocked all contact, but now that he was trapped by those Earthling overlords, she was more open to receiving his messages.

Sighing unhappily, she indicated that he was

overloading her senses, and immediately felt him calm a little as he thanked her for hearing him. "So! What is it you need me to know, Commander?"

"The warmongers who have captured me expect me to help them find some sort of dangerous material they say you are involved with. Does this make sense?"

"Yes. It will be the professor's work they are referring to."

"What is it? What did he discover?"

"The professor developed a powder, a material that holds interdimensional properties."

"I see! That's why they are so concerned."

"The professor wanted the whole world to benefit from the magical nature of this material, for he seemed to know that the Earthling world was about to experience an alteration in frequency levels so the development of this powder was designed to assist in a collective raising of consciousness."

"Ah … much is now making sense."

"Before he died, the professor perfected the production of the powder and an acquaintance—an Earthling I once met—has stored it somewhere in his city."

"Is this man called Jimmy White?"

"No, no! Jim may know something about where it is hidden, but he does not have it."

"These Earthlings think he does."

Chaldee paused, suddenly concerned for the friends she had left in Sydney. "What do they want of you, Commander? What are they saying?"

"I'm supposed to find where this man has stored the material."

"I am not sure what your intentions are, Commander, but what they ask of you is incorrect. A group I have had limited contact with has stored the material somewhere, but Mr. White is unaware of its location." Chaldee paused, wondering how she could influence this old warrior. "Commander, you must not submit to their demands. It will end in disaster. I advise you to befriend Mr. White. Help him. Tell him what you have told me. Trust that your effort will be rewarded."

"Am I exonerated?"

"No, Commander, there will still be a trial when you return, but all the circumstances will be taken into consideration."

"Your words will aid my decision, Madame, but that is all I will say. These humans have interesting offers also."

Chaldee could feel the contact being broken so hurriedly she reached out, imploringly: "I advise you to return, Commander, you belong here." But even as she sent the message, she knew he was gone. So, what would he do? Although he was an old man now, completely banished from their community, he was still her subject; she still was responsible for his well-being.

Frowning, Chaldee stood at the cave entrance, gazing across the valley, remembering when it was a dense forest, remembering how the Commander had tried to take control, remembering how life was then as compared to now, and in a sweet moment of insight Chaldee realized she had much to be thankful for. The sanctuary here was safe, her people were still united, and the future looked hopeful. With a feeling of strange expectation Chaldee went out into the main cave asking that her Master Speaker join her out beyond the entrance. When he appeared, Zell seemed flustered. "I am sorry, Madame, but there has been a minor upheaval in Aegeus's area. The scientist was experimenting with Professor Egeland's powder and somehow it caused a small rupture in the rockface."

"Really!" Chaldee was startled. Maybe this was the reason for her vision of an earthquake. "What was he trying to do?"

"He believes that we can connect our mind to this substance, Madame, but he has not yet found a safe method."

Chaldee smiled, for she was very fond of the young crippled scientist. "I am sure his experiments will eventually succeed, Zell, and such advancement will be beneficial." She paused, waiting for her Master Speaker to speak, but he seemed satisfied that there was nothing to fear. "But we have many other problems to deal with, Zell."

Chaldee was still deep in a conversation with her Master Speaker when she received an odd message from Enka, telling her that someone was coming to get some of the professor's powder: but even as Enka's message was still drawing her attention, she began to notice a shimmering light in the cave. She paused, waving at Zell to be still, watching intently as a vague form begin to manifest.

"I … I bid you welcome," Chaldee whispered in an uncertain voice as she watched the air flicker and dance in front of her.

"My Lady, it is a pleasure." Although vague and wispy, the figure was now fully formed.

Chaldee could see this apparition was extremely tall and very thin. His head was large but what took most of her attention was the radiant blue of his eyes. Chaldee took a deep, rather shocked breath. "Again, sir, I say you are welcome here, though I do not understand your business with us, or indeed, who you might be."

"We will discuss me later, but I am here to explain that your young ensign, Enka, is about to send you a warning, but although Paul has had an accident, my people can help if you give permission."

"Paul!" Chaldee was on her feet immediately. "What has happened?"

"My Lady, do not fear. He will recover if you allow us to intervene."

"Who are you?" the Master Speaker demanded.

"Our home is in the inner Earth, and we have all the facilities needed to restore his health, but you, too, can give aid. You have healing material here that will help his recovery."

Chaldee shook her head trying to grasp the fullness of who he was and what he was telling her about Paul.

"We have equipment that will transfer him off the ledge, but I am here to ask if we can use your powder."

"The professor's powder?" The Master Speaker's frown showed his uncertainty.

"I believe it will help heal his wounds."

Chaldee was trying not to panic, but her hand twisted in knots as she whispered: "You said ledge; has Paul fallen? You must sit … please … tell me what has happened."

The stranger pulled a chair across, so he was sitting directly in front of Chaldee. He took one of her hands as he began to describe how Paul's fall had broken his leg, injured his back, and had caused a severe headwound. "It happened because the cave wall collapsed, and he fell."

"This is terrible!" Chaldee clutched at his hand.

"At present, he is still unconscious and is laying on a ledge, but the one you call Joe is with him, supporting him."

"Sir … your … your explanation is …" Chaldee's voice trailed away, as she struggled to understand.

"You say the powder will help with the healing?" the Master Speaker asked sharply. "How do you know about the professor's material?"

The stranger glanced at the Master Speaker. "Sir, we

have been aware of your presence ever since the alignment drew you into these caves."

The Master Speaker was shocked. "I see … so you know who we are?"

The stranger nodded.

"I see," Zell repeated, now as confused as Chaldee. "Then … it … it is safe to take the powder?"

"Indeed, sir, we have no intention of abusing the privilege. We are aware of how important this material is. Our people were impressed by the powerful mind of the professor who developed it. We can only guess at the benefits this powder will make possible. So, of course, we would like to work with it … with your permission."

The Master Speaker seemed reassured by the stranger's obvious respect for the professor's work. "So how much powder will be needed? We have packed it in small containers."

"Just a container to start with, although we would be grateful for any you care to give us."

"Zell, we must ask Aegeus to pack up a few boxes for it is important to share the professor's work." Chaldee stood up, bowing slightly to this tall, wafer-thin stranger. "I am mystified by who you are, sir! Amazed by what you know, but I give full permission for any assistance you can offer Paul." Chaldee watched as her Master Speaker hurried away. "I feel confident of your help, but I insist that I be there. I must see him."

"Enka is still at the site."

Chaldee nodded. "I will tell him to wait … and I will come at once."

As the stranger stood up, Chaldee noticed how his entire form seemed to waver, almost disappearing in the dim light. "Could you tell me your name? What race do you belong to?"

"I am known as Isaak and I come from an inner-Earth civilization. We are human, a part of humanity who left this surface atmosphere long ago."

"I see, so you find this density difficult?"

The tall man nodded. "My people are multidimensional, and although we do find this frequency challenging, I am pleased to have a reason to come to the surface, for the more I work within this dense atmosphere, the more profound my experience becomes."

Chaldee's gaze was thoughtful. Here was a being who might have some understanding of her mission, but she did not have time for further pondering as Zell and the crippled scientist Aegeus reappeared.

"I have two containers here," Aegeus said. "I hope this will be enough."

Isaak nodded. "I am grateful, but reality is flowing quickly, and your compatriot is in urgent need of help." Isaak took Chaldee's hand again. "I will expect to see you again very soon, Princess Chaldee, and I am most pleased we have had this meeting at long last." He smiled and disappeared before Chaldee could answer.

As Chaldee gave last-minute instruction to Zell, Waldus, the handmaiden who had always served Chaldee, quickly prepared a small backpack of food and equipment. Then calling for Patch and Aegeus to go with her, Chaldee swiftly entered the cave system. She was sure that Patch would guide them. He was one of the older palace guards and had been protecting her since she was a small child. She was a little concerned that Aegeus might not keep up because of his crippled leg but he knew more about the powder than she did, so he must be part of this exploration.

As they struggled through the treacherous terrain, Enka occasionally sent telepathic messages. He said he could not see the ledge below very clearly, but it seemed as if Joe was working on Paul, then a little later he described how a small, noiseless machine had just risen up from the depths and had carefully removed Paul, and that Joe was about to climb up from the ledge.

As they hurried on, Chaldee relayed these confusing messages to Patch and Aegeus, but despite all their efforts it was many hours before they reached the site of the collapse. Enka was there waiting, and with him was another very tall, fragile light-being, whose shimmering appearance was similar to Isaak's. Chaldee greeted them, thankful to have arrived.

"This is Abe," Enka said as he guided Chaldee over to the newcomer. "He was a great help as they moved Paul off the ledge."

Chaldee offered her hand to Abe. "We thank you, sir … and where is Paul now?"

"He has been moved to our city, My Lady. He will be well cared for."

Chaldee glance was searching as she monitored Abe's thoughts.

"Trust us, Princess Chaldee, he will be well cared for."

Chaldee smiled as she recognized Abe's telepathic ability, then she glanced across to where Joe sat hunched up against the rockface. "What is the matter, Joe?"

Joe shrugged but did not answer, but Enka said in a restrained voice: "Joe feels he is to blame."

"It was an accident, Joe," Chaldee said kindly, then stepped a little closer to the massive hole, squinting into the blackened space.

Immediately Patch pulled her back. "Take care, Princess," he growled.

"You say it was a boulder that caused this calamity," Chaldee asked Joe as she allowed Patch to pull her away.

Joe nodded miserably.

Chaldee briefly touched Joe's shoulder. "Do not be so harsh with yourself."

"Exactly," Abe said. "Joe could not have known why or how the boulder had been placed there. It is nobody's fault. Many generations ago my people placed a large boulder here and over time it would have weakened the wall. Their idea was to block the path of anyone who tried to enter our domain."

Joe's face brightened a little as he listened.

"… and they used a type of drone to lift Paul off the ledge." Excitedly Enka broke across Abe's words. "And, Madame, Abe will show us another way of entering into their domain. He has been explaining a little about their kingdom. They are very advanced."

Chaldee smiled weakly, still surprised by the revelation of this underworld race. "I am grateful."

The tall being bowed low. "Princess Chaldee, our people will be excited to have you visit. When you are ready, I'd be honored to take you to them. There is a hidden ramp farther along this tunnel."

Chaldee smiled. "Of course." Then turned her attention back to Joe, who was struggling to his feet. "Joe, tell me what happened down there on the ledge … how did you help Paul?"

"It was the powder, Chaldee … did you give it to Isaak?"

Chaldee nodded.

"Well, it's as weird as anything else that has happened," Joe said in amazement. "I was trying to figure out what to do. The area was so small it was hard to keep my balance, and there was blood everywhere …" Joe paused. "Then suddenly I had this voice in my head telling me how to use the powder … then a container was pushed into my hand … but I couldn't see anybody!"

"It would have been Isaak," Abe explained. "He had obtained the material from you, Madame."

Chaldee nodded again.

"And the ledge is very small, Joe, so he would have simply remained outside, helping you that way," Abe continued.

"Well, I didn't see anybody," Joe said thoughtfully. "The stuff was just shoved in my hand and this voice told me how to use it. I had to take one pinch at a time and dust it across Paul's leg. Jeez! It was a terrible mess! I had to try to straighten his leg. It was twisted underneath him; it was bleeding and badly broken." Joe paused wiping his face. "It was bad, Chaldee. Anyway, this voice told me how to straighten the leg and use the powder and this seemed to stop the bleeding. Then I was told to do the same thing to the cut across his forehead, and that also helped." Joe stopped, for the first time looking straight at Chaldee. "He was badly hurt, yet the powder seemed to help immediately. I can't explain how … but, Chaldee, this powder is miraculous. Anyway, I watched as they moved him onto the drone … and he really did seem a little better."

Chaldee smiled. "You did well."

Joe bowed his head but did not answer.

"But you must tell us more, Joe," Aegeus pleaded. "I have been experimenting with this material and have found it has properties that seem almost to defy dimensions."

Joe frowned. "What do you mean?"

"After making many mistakes, I realized that to achieve the result I was seeking I had to merge my mind with the powder. I had to visualize an outcome as if I was part of the process! Sometimes it worked, sometimes it didn't, so I know there is still much to learn."

Thoughtfully Joe looked at Aegeus. "Well … yes … Isaak told me to focus and imagine that Paul was healing."

"Right." Aegeus clapped his hands in excitement: "Exactly so. Exactly so!"

"I sort of forgot that … things were bad down there,

Aegeus. Paul's blood was everywhere … he was moaning … in pain …"

"But you did as you were asked. You altered your consciousness until you were in harmony with the elements of the powder."

"What does this mean?" Chaldee asked, trying to remain calm, although she was affected by Aegeus's excitement.

"As I say, I have been doing a lot of work with this amazing material, and I think it has components or factors that move across dimensions. Maybe it uses our electrical fields or our cellular biology to link with our focus." Aegeus paused then whispered, "Or maybe we have to merge with it!"

"Are you saying it's alive?" Enka demanded, his eyes wide as he began to understand what was being said.

"Ah … well, yes. This material is certainly adding to our understanding of consciousness," Abe said gravely.

"I see." Chaldee looked from Joe to Aegeus. "You have both been part of something really profound. I am amazed by the professor's wisdom. He knew exactly where his experiment was leading, but I do not think he understood the upheaval his creation would cause."

Aegeus nodded.

Joe shrugged as if to heave a pressure off his shoulders. "I think Paul will be okay, Chaldee."

"Then perhaps, if we are all in agreement, we could get started," Abe coaxed.

Without another word, everybody picked up their gear and began to traipse after Abe, taking care as the passageway narrowed and began to slope downward. As the descent became steep, they found they had to brace themselves against the sides of the rock walls. Eventually Abe stopped, and pushing aside another large stone he led them onto what appeared to be a type of ramp, or bridge. Their helmet lights were not powerful enough to show exactly where they were, but Chaldee felt they were crossing over water. Eventually they reached an area that seemed a little lighter, and ahead Chaldee could see a faint bluish glow.

"Is that a light up ahead, Abe?" Joe asked excitedly.

"Yes," Abe said simply. "We are nearly home."

Part Two
Desperate Politics

Chapter One
Jake Is Warned

Jake's height and mop of curly hair often caused him to stand out in a crowd, but these days he had become like a shadow, always careful, always hidden. He guessed he was on some sort of official "persons of interest" list because of the deadly incident at the mine over a year ago, when he had accidently shot Martin. It had been a traumatic event, especially as both he and Paul had thought of Martin as their friend when in fact the man was really working as an undercover agent, so these days Jake was very careful. He made sure nobody knew where he lived; he moved constantly; his phone was always disconnected—unless he was using it—and he had reduced his contacts to a select few as he tried to shore up his life. The terrible events in Broken Hill had alerted Jake to the highly informed, strategically hidden governmental network, so he made sure they had no idea where he was.

Now, amid the dying light of the day, Jake was being particularly careful. He had received a message from somebody who obviously knew the old system, but he had no idea whether they were friend or foe, so he felt wary and apprehensive. As he inched forward, he saw the long, menacing shadow of a person hiding behind a dilapidated factory wall, so he moved back, waiting and watching. Nothing moved or was heard—except the chirping of birds heralding the closing of the day. He glanced behind but the road was empty. It seemed nobody was here, except himself and whoever was hiding behind the wall. He knew the place had not been used for years, and the area concealing the stranger was leaning at a precarious angle, so he wondered who would want to take this risk but on the other hand the strange e-mail he received had certainly forced him to take the gamble.

His entire group was under extreme pressure because of Professor Egeland's formula. The old physicist had died before he could fully test his work, so Chaldee had suggested they hold off from releasing it to the world until Aegeus understood the full extent of its power; the stuff obviously meant something to somebody. From the moment Jake had been asked to protect the old scientist, he realized just how influential Professor Egeland's work would eventually be, but he never expected this blustering nonsense. The present intimidation had started with flashy offers of money, but those enormous sums simply warned him that this material was important. After the bribes came the threats, and the game suddenly became very dark indeed. Jake knew they were dealing with a dangerous force, and today's meeting here in this old factory complex had come about because somebody somewhere was extending a warning, but Jake was fully aware of the danger, so he took a step back, feeling it might be better to abort rather than face what was waiting for him. Then suddenly the figure stepped out into the light and Jake relaxed as he realized it was old Billy Jacobs, once a Tasmanian forestry protester.

"Billy! What are you doing here?" Jake was amazed. "Was it you who sent that e-mail?"

Billy grinned. "I betcha didn't think I could use one of them technical computer thingys, eh!"

Jake took the older man by the arm leading him into a small office inside the abandoned factory. "I'm really pleased to see you, but what are you doing here? Who sent you? The e-mail seemed to be offering help."

Billy took a breath that ended in a bout of coughing, collapsing into a dusty chair as he tried to breathe. "I know a bit about what's going on, Jake. News filters through."

Jake nodded, watching, waiting, wondering how this old man could be of any help.

"That documentary you guys aired has knocked us all for a six … amazing stuff!"

"Yeah, it's caused a bit of a stir."

"More than that, Jakey boy. It's starting a whole new global movement … it's radical, mate, radical." As he spoke, Billy leaned over punching Jake lightly on the arm. "But that's not why I'm here."

"No?"

The old man glanced around the small room. "Is it safe in here?"

"There're no bugs if that's what you mean," Jake answered.

"Hmm." Billy did not seem convinced.

"It's why I suggested this place, because it's safe."

"If you say so, Jake." Billy scratched his balding head. "Have to be careful … ah … I may have upset a few guys … if you get my meaning."

Jake frowned. "What's happened?"

"It's to do with that material your guys have stashed away."

"What are you talking about?"

Old Billy drew another sharp breath, coughing a little as he settled back in his chair. "When I saw that doco … the part about the professor's work … it rang a few bells, so I got in touch with a couple of mates … old boffins who used to work at the CSIRO."

"I remember … that's where you worked."

"Once," Billy said tersely. "Anyway, over the years I've kept in touch, so I rang them asking about your so-called powder."

"Really!" Suddenly Jake felt anxious, knowing instinctively that this was why the old man was being so cautious. "I bet you weren't welcome."

"Yeah, you're right about that. Stirred up a heap of muck, mate," Billy muttered, then grinned across at Jake. "But what's new!"

Jake's smile was grim. "We are having similar problems."

"Well, I'm not surprised. You know what that powder seems to be, don't you?"

"According to Professor Egeland's papers, it has dynamic potential."

"Absolutely, mate. It's amazing. Too powerful for you guys to simply give it out to the world. The Yanks have something similar … with antigravity properties although an icy temperature is part of their system and from what I can make out, your material is different because it doesn't have those limitations."

Jake shook his head, suddenly feeling stupid.

"Your professor has pushed you guys into the quantum field, mate! At a very sophisticated level from what my boffins say." Billy squinted at Jake. "They said … ah … that stuff very similar to the professor's design is being used in quantum computers, in aerospace; they're even playing around with AI and parallel worlds, Jake … so can you see why your work is so important."

Jake didn't answer but he was shocked.

"And, of course, it's an amazing weapon … yet you people think it's some sort of panacea, with the power to heal." Billy stopped, suddenly out of breath.

"I know it's powerful, that's why it belongs to everybody."

Billy smiled as he shook his head. "I love you guys, I really do, but you can't be this naïve. What you have is extraordinary. It's a threat to a very powerful set of people,

Jake. Warmongers. Tycoons. Blokes who think they rule the world and believe me … they do not like what you are doing."

"Chaldee says the professor's discovery can resonate at different levels. Apparently, it functions across dimensions. It can work with one's thought processes in a sort of harmonic vibration and assist in balancing left and right brain patterns, but she never mentioned any of your stuff."

"Yeah … yeah … of course it can be used for good. It could solve the entire world's energy problems if they would allow it, but they won't … this is why I am here … to warn you. Your powder is revolutionary, mate. I know this stuff sounds unreal but from what they are telling me, I think it might be some sort of superconductor. Believe me, Jake, they will stop you any way they can!"

Jake stared at the old man, slowly shaking his head. He could hear the caution in Billy's voice, could see the fear in his eyes, so he knew the warning was very real, but also he remembered the danger Professor Egeland had faced. "The material the professor created has always been for the people, Billy. His work was absolutely cutting edge. He said his research was controversial, that's why we had to help him in the first place; why Chaldee's people took him in. These goons knew what he was developing even back then. It's why they were trying to stop him—but they never did. We can't quit now. It's the same old game."

"You won't make it, matey, … they're always in control."

"Not according to Chaldee."

The old man ran a wrinkled hand across his face, shaking his head in despair. "Don't argue, Jake. They'll stop you. One way or another, they'll end it, and I don't want you to get hurt. That's why I'm here."

"You're doing the same thing, Billy! You're trying to stop us."

"Yeah … but for your own good!"

"Crickey, mate," Jake yelled. "I'm not in this for my own good … I want the professor's work to have some kind of positive impact!"

Billy cocked his head on one side and for a long time he just stared at Jake, then he said quietly: "Well … there's a bloke I know about … a physicist … and I think he would be a bit interested in what you've got."

"How'd ya mean?"

"A few years back he was toying with some of the inventions Nicola Tesla had been developing … he's working on some sort of power system so he might be worth reaching out to … name's Dr. Ralph Miller."

"Interesting."

"Yeah … well, you need to do more than just hand this stuff around, Jake, you want to get other people involved, too."

Immediately Jake was on the alert. "Who sent you … do they know you're here?"

"No … no … but they know about me … that's why I intend to disappear … booked a flight back to Hobart tonight," Billy whispered. "Then I'm gone … they'll never find me down there."

Jake smiled at the idea of this old man fading into the forest. Of course, they would never find him.

"But I'm here to warn you," Billy continued. "I know you won't listen, but I had to try because you and your team are in deep trouble. Does that guy Jim White know you are being threatened?"

"Jim's having the same trouble, but as I say, they'll not stop us."

"Where's the stuff being stored?"

Jake looked at Billy, his eyes narrowed. "It's in a warehouse—safe," he said sharply.

"Okay … okay … I'm not spying. As I say, I'm just here to warn you."

Jake shrugged.

"Right then … I guess this is all I can do. The rest is up to you."

Jake was noncommittal.

"Okay … but don't forget to get in touch with Dr. Miller, he's in Melbourne now." Billy shrugged and there was a long helpless pause.

Jake knew the old fighter was trying to help, but he also knew Chaldee's abilities. His faith was in her and in the work Professor Egeland had completed.

"Okay, mate, best we go, I don't want to miss the plane. Can you give me a lift back to town?"

"I've got a bike, a motor bike, will that do?"

The old man nodded, and the two rebels cautiously moved out into the open space in front of the buildings. Jake was always careful, like a phantom, hardly ever seen unless he wanted it, and now because of what old Billy had said, he felt particularly vulnerable.

Chapter Two
Trials and Tribulations

Senator Jim White had flown in from Canberra to meet Jake and was now waiting in the bar of their local pub. Absently he sat, holding his drink, retracing the events of the day. For months he had tried to hide his fury at the political dithering regarding the science of climate change so today he had tabled a private member's bill that outlined a radical program that addressed methods of working with the ravages of nature. This private member's bill was a very formal document written up by a parliamentary council, so the content had demanded all of Jim's attention. The proposed legislation would examine ways to repatriate many drought- and fire-affected communities by designing and building protected townships; by incorporating more advanced farming practices; by developing commercial methods to create water; by seriously considering the ramification of sea rise; by developing underground facilities right across the country; and by attempting to incorporate the innovative material Chaldee's professor had developed. The bill had been debated today and the negative response was even worse than Jim had expected. Eventually he lost his temper, launching into a tirade that had him ejected from the chamber for twenty-four hours.

Now as he glumly sat reviewing the day's debacle,

Jim wondered if Jake might be a person he could talk to. Jake was much younger and had been part of his daughter Adele's life since secondary college, and although the boy had dropped out of university and appeared to be some type of activist, Jim still regarded the younger man as someone with integrity—and that's what he needed right now.

Jim had ordered their meals and was halfway through his steak when Jake slid into the seat opposite.

"Sorry I'm late. Had to take a bloke over to the airport." Jake heaved his elbows onto the table.

"You don't sound happy … what's up?" Although Jim was trying to sound normal, his rage still burned.

"Well, you look like I feel," Jake laughed as he pulled an untouched meal in front of him. "I guess this is mine."

Jim nodded. "I've had a bad day, but what happened to you?"

Jake paused and it seemed as if he was searching for the right words. "Well … this afternoon I met an old guy I used to know when I was in Tasmania. He seemed a bit intense … wanted to warn me about the professor's material … said we were challenging death or words to that effect."

"But Adele said the professor had perfected his discovery," Jim protested.

"No, no … not the powder … it's the mob demanding we hand the stuff over. They're the threat. Old Billy reckons the powder's a sort of superconductor or something, and we are upsetting the very rich and powerful … per usual." Jake shrugged and turned his attention to his food.

Jim frowned. "Maybe it has something to do with that weird offer I got? A million dollars for both the stock and patent—but it was an offer, not a threat."

"Yeah, well, Billy reckons these guys are powerful and we should do as they ask," Jake said thoughtfully.

"Anyway, you've turned them down ... haven't you?"

Jim nodded. "Of course. What does Chaldee think?"

"I haven't heard from them for weeks."

"That reminds me," Jim said, trying not to seem preoccupied. "There's a rumor going around Canberra that the army or the police or somebody has one of Chaldee's men."

"What?"

"I couldn't make any sense of it, so I'm not sure if it's true, but just suppose it's right," Jim said quietly.

"Wow! That's not good ... imagine what they will try to do to that poor guy."

"I supposed he has the same power as Chaldee." Jim attempted a half-hearted laugh. "I mean ... he could cause some real damage if he got going."

"I guess so," Jake said automatically, his glance now fixed on Jim's face. "But you don't sound happy. What's wrong?"

"Ah ... I don't know, Jake. I don't think I can do this for much longer."

Jake waved his fork in the air, waiting for a clearer explanation.

"They debated my bill today ... it was much worse than I expected and eventually they kicked me out."

"Thrown out ... of ... parliament? Crickey!"

"They ejected me for twenty-four hours," Jim said with a short bitter laugh. "For telling them we had to act urgently because the change in our climate is at crisis level; that immediate long-range planning is absolutely necessary if we are going to keep the population safe."

"So, did they reject your bill?"

Jim nodded. "It was a bad day ... to be quite honest I don't know exactly what words I used I was so angry."

Jake nodded sympathetically.

"Anyway, I don't know whether to resign."

Jake made a soundless whistle. "I know how much

work you put into developing that bill, Jim, but resigning's not the answer."

"I've got to get some sort of action started … real action involving scientists, social planners, farmers, the union movement … a whole group of leaders."

Jake put down his fork, staring excitedly at Jim. "That's the type of stuff will get people stirred up. Maybe forget trying to use parliament … if you're clever about how you word it all, most people will listen. We voted you in because of what you were proposing, so you've the right credentials … and you're building up a following …"

Jim smiled at Jake's enthusiasm. "It'd be absolutely legitimate. An organized group who would offer real planning strategies."

As Jake was about to answer, Jim's phone beeped. It was a message from Adele in London.

"Hi, Dad. I'm coming home."

Adele was waiting at Sydney airport, unaware of the drama taking place in Chaldee's world, and equally unaware of the dangers that had begun to surround Jake and her father. She had left a message for Jake before she boarded the plane at Heathcote, as she knew he only checked his phone once a day, and she needed him to be there when she got off the plane.

She had been touring the country for six months, giving talks and showing her documentary to many eager audiences. People often kept her after the lecture wanting to know more about Chaldee, about this magical princess and her kingdom. Also, they asked about the professor's powder, wondering when it would be distributed. Adele described Chaldee's lovely palace, or what it was like before it was destroyed, explaining how this unknown race was now without a home. People wondered if Princess Chaldee could offer any help to mankind, sympathizing with Adele's outrage as she spoke of the heavy hand of her government and the way Chaldee's kingdom had been eliminated.

Adele's excitement when speaking about this race of advanced people could always be heard as she described her own change since knowing Chaldee, outlining her new, although undeveloped, telepathic abilities and how such skills could be learned by anybody. She was grateful because of how information in the documentary was starting to influence people worldwide, and when their questions turned to the powder it seemed that already this material was being linked to myths like the Golden Fleece or the Philosopher's Stone.

Deucallus often accompanied her, answering questions about Chaldee and also himself, though he would never speak about his own group, secure in a hidden and remote area high in the Andes. When challenged by the question of climate change, Deucallus stated in exasperation that these Earth changes were cyclic. He stated calmly that the planet had always been in flux, that the changes occurring now had happened many times before, but despite the many scientific claims and archaeological discoveries he warned that ordinary people were still unaware of the truth.

After knowing Deucallus for only a few days—when they were together in Sydney—Adele had realized he had an understanding far beyond her own, so she began to examine his claims and found that experts had provable data showing the planet had begun to warm long before the increase in greenhouse gases; that the drama did appear to be cyclic as Deucallus was claiming. These heated arguments often went on long after the lecture had ended, and Deucallus always had an answer.

As her tour continued, Adele became aware that the power of social media was distorting information, and this was starting to damage her presentation. Deucallus warned that her anger was causing her to become overly emotional and although she tried to remain calm, her passion, coupled with the amazing candor found in her documentary, caused Adele's presence to be noted by governmental intelligence. She would use emotion to remind people how governments across the world were failing to put strategies in place that would safeguard the population against extreme weather, against the extinction of species and rising public awareness and the confrontations this was causing. As she spoke to audiences across Britain, Adele's disquiet was unmistakable, for the social upheaval she saw everywhere made her despair for the future.

But it was on her day off in Bath City that Adele had firsthand experience of the danger Deucallus had been warning her about. Luxuriating as a happy tourist after giving an exhausting lecture the night before, Adele had spent most of the morning wandering around the city. As she sat in a tiny café drinking coffee, two American girls about her own age approached. They recognized and congratulated her on the work she was doing, speaking enthusiastically about their own plans to start a new community when they got home. When they suggested she go with them on a site-seeing tour of Wells Cathedral, Adele did not hesitate. To be with friends, away from the worry and responsibility, even for a day, was a relief.

It was not a long drive to the small township of Wells, but as they arrived it started to rain. Adele was not concerned. The area was beautiful despite the weather. As she stood on the grass, gazing through the mist at the west front of the cathedral, Adele was totally overwhelmed by its majesty. The medieval carvings were exquisite, and the layout of the facade so breathtaking she could not help but liken this superb building to some of the wonders she had seen in Chaldee's palace.

Completely transfixed, Adele walked slowly through the drizzling rain toward the entrance. Suddenly she realized that her two American friends had disappeared. Puzzled she looked around. How could the girls have left without a word? Almost at the same moment she noticed people pointing at a small drone circling low over the grass. Adele was dismayed seeing such ugliness within the grounds of this beautiful place, but it also worried her that the disappearance of the girls had occurred almost at the same time as this drone appeared. Frowning, Adele hurried out of the grayness of the late afternoon, very aware of the safety the cathedral offered, but once inside, the breathtaking beauty of the architecture swept away all her worries. Slowly she moved down toward the scissored archway, staring up at the roof above the nave almost unable to believe the glory of what she was seeing. Adele was astonished by how such an ancient people had created this miracle, letting her mind drift back over the centuries to a time when designers and builders spent generations creating such masterpieces right across Christendom. It held a similar feeling of perfection to what she had felt wandering around Chaldee's palace and as she compared the two, she wondered how the people would feel if suddenly the army came marching in and destroyed this cathedral? She found a seat, allowing the hushed calm to wrap her in a momentary peace.

It was almost dark when Adele emerged from the cathedral. The light rain of earlier had now become a wild storm. The torrential rain was like a river pouring from the sky, and the wind had become a banshee screaming around the building. Sheltered by the cathedral's doorway, Adele was appalled. She had no umbrella, the girls with the car had disappeared, and Deucallus was in Edinburgh organizing the next showing of the documentary, so she had no idea of what to do. Already she could see the cathedral lawn beginning to flood. With a helpless groan, she decided to run over to where she last saw the car. Maybe they were still there; but as she neared the car park, she realized it, too, was flooding. With no idea of where she could go, Adele had begun to traipse back to the cathedral when two hooded figures loomed up out of the deluge. She knew immediately she was in danger, but there was nowhere to run.

"You've got a big mouth, lady," one hood had yelled, grabbing her by the shoulders. "You need to watch what you say! That stuff of yours is so crazy, you are upsetting everybody!"

"You're crazy, all right," the other hooded figure had screeched as he punched her in the stomach. "You better quit now. Go back to Australia … otherwise, we'll make sure something nasty happens."

Adele had no idea how many times she was hit. She had fallen into the wet dirt as the two men repeatedly pummeled and kicked her. Eventually, when they seemed to have gone, she tried to sit up, but the world turned to gray. The next few hours were full of pain and confusion. Somebody found her laying in the mud, bloody and unconscious. The ambulance took her to hospital, and after a long night of trauma she eventually regained some sense of reality.

Eventually Adele spent nearly a week in hospital recuperating. Deucallus canceled the gigs in Scotland, returning to St Martin's hospital in time to take Adele back to London, where she promptly decided to pack up and return to Sydney.

Deucallus was puzzled as to why she was in Wells. Why go there? His question led Adele to retrace her movements. She remembered that the two American girls who drove her there had disappeared. They had suggested the cathedral; they had led her into the trap, but she had no idea who they were. Then she remembered talking about the cathedral's beauty in one of her lectures. Somehow her movements had been choreographed by someone intent on making a serious statement and that drone must have been part of it. Deucallus said it was obvious that the documentary was ruffling feathers somewhere, agreeing that they should quit for the time being. The viciousness of Adele's beating was a warning, but Deucallus was not sure who had instigated it. Obviously, powerful people were upset by what Adele was presenting, and while he had no idea who they might be, he understood why.

Chapter Three
Robert McCloud's Politics

The Commander had spent a few restless days in the small house McCloud had called a "unit." It was very high above the ground, with a design that squeezed all the other units into one large block. This, he decided, was overwhelmingly ugly, and he had no idea why builders would create such restrictive dwellings. He had not seen his two jailors since they planted him there, but they had left the driver as both a support and a guardian. This driver delivered food every few hours and appeared to be standing guard outside the main door.

The Commander had explored the entire unit, liking the comfort of the furniture, especially the bed, but irritated by how small the place was. He found little interest in the object that beamed out pictures and information, but he was drawn to the lilting music coming from another box hidden in a drawer. These were sounds he had never heard before, and he wondered how the Earthling had created such a beautifully harmonic structure. These people continued to amaze him.

Eventually the Commander was able to convince the driver to take him back to the ocean. The sight of such an exquisite landscape had not left him, and he was longing to return, but once there he found the heat unbearable. He could not stay on the sand for very long, but each time he ventured down to the water's edge he was overcome by emotion. The vibrancy at this point was amazing. To be standing at the edge of this huge land mass feeling the power of the flowing water was exhilarating. As he gazed across the glittering blue of sky and sea, the Commander's delight soared to such a point that at one stage, he could feel himself lifting off the sand. Levitating like this because of such heightened emotion was extraordinary. It had been many years since he had been so affected. Time and time again he would return to the edge, gazing into the water's cascading geometric patterns as it flowed onto the land, but always the sting of the sun forced him back into the shade. At one stage he took note of how many humans were stretched out in the heat. How could they bear it?

Eventually the Commander saw Robert McCloud approaching. The Earthling's formal dress, complete with dark tie, seemed conspicuously out of place, but the deputy secretary did not seem to notice.

"This is an odd place to find you," McCloud said sarcastically. "Down here among the seagulls."

"This is the most exciting area I have experienced since arriving in your city." The Commander dramatically threw his arms wide. "Here, at the juncture of land and water, one can feel the most exuberant energy!"

"Really." McCloud cocked his head on one side, unable to comprehend what was being said.

"The feeling one has when standing here is beyond my ability to explain."

McCloud still appeared puzzled.

"Do you not realize, sir, that at the point where these two energy fields merge—at the water's edge—there is such an upswing of power it can lift one off one's feet!"

Robert McCloud grinned, and his driver shrugged

offhandedly. "If you say so, Commander, but I think you might also benefit from a visit to Canberra … to our parliament. That's why I'm here."

The Commander was not at all interested. Nothing was going to take him away from this euphoric energy. "I shall stay here."

"Sorry, sir, we need to move on. There is much you need to learn if you are going to help us."

"I will stay here until I feel the to urge to move." Robert McCloud appeared peeved, so the Commander changed the subject. "I can see this wonderland does not attract you, but I have more disturbing news, so let me add to your discomfort." The Commander glanced sharply at both men, before looking around for somewhere to sit.

"Do you drink coffee?" McCloud asked.

The Commander shook his head slightly. "I do not think so, but I will try."

"Good." McCloud crossed the footpath, seating himself at the table of the small sea-front café ordering coffee before turning his attention back to the Commander.

"So … what is it you must tell me?"

The Commander settled into his chair, pleased to be in the shade, but not quite sure how he should phrase Chaldee's news about the tsunami.

They sat in silence until the coffee came.

"As I say … the information I must convey might disturb you."

Robert McCloud shrugged.

"I have been told that in the very near future this beautiful place will be washed over by what you Earthlings call a tidal wave."

McCloud frowned and scratched his ear. "What do you mean?"

"There will be an earthquake somewhere out in the ocean beyond this land."

"Rubbish … who told you that?"

"It will create a tsunami that will devastate many South Pacific lands and will certainly wash away the northern areas of your coast."

McCloud stared at the Commander over his coffee cup. "You're joking, of course."

The Commander did not answer, for as he read McCloud's mind, he could see that this Earthling was trying hard to deny the concern he was suddenly feeling. "I know you believe me, so you must inform your authorities. They need to begin to move the population away from your northern shores."

"You can't be serious, man. How could I suddenly drop such a bombshell? I mean … who would listen? How would I convince them?"

It was the Commander's turn to shrug.

"You obviously got this absurd information from that woman!"

"Princess Chaldee does have the ability to move beyond the structures of third-dimensional time … yes."

"No! It's nonsense … and I won't listen."

"I think the rising of new land is imminent, but you must decide what to do." The Commander stood up. "And I do not like your coffee … thank you." He stared down at Robert McCloud. "Now I will return to the meeting of the energy fields."

McCloud watched the Commander hobble back across the sand toward the water's edge, wondering whether this alien being was giving him warning of a catastrophe or maybe it was an old man's fantasy. He shook his head, refusing to admit that there might be truth in what that woman had forecast. He realized that as deputy secretary of the army he had a duty to speak up, but how could he? They would laugh him out of the department. Maybe he could send an anonymous e-mail or drop a note on somebody's desk.

The next morning Robert McCloud made sure he had the Commander in the car, secure and safe, heading toward the airport. He wanted this strange man to observe Jim White as he presented his private member's bill. Nobody expected White to be victorious, but the bill had been prepared and today it would be debated. By putting the Commander in the public gallery McCloud was sure the old man would gain the type of information Skip had requested. Robert McCloud was not sure who wanted such information or why, but he knew that Jimmy White was becoming a problem, and this was the perfect opportunity to dig deeper into who the politician was working for.

McCloud could see that the Commander was sitting forward on his seat, his hands clenching and unclenching as the car forced its way through the heavy morning traffic. Then later as they strapped themselves in for the flight to Canberra, it seemed the crazy old man was almost as anxious on the plane.

"I am very much afraid that this flimsy flying machine is about to fall out of the sky," the Commander complained, not seeming to care how ridiculous he sounded.

Eventually they landed in Canberra and were met by Skip Warner and another secret service officer. McCloud kept a close watch on the Commander, who seemed preoccupied as they all gathered around a table for more coffee.

The Commander had been terrified in the plane, but now that they were safely on the ground, he was amusing himself by checking the minds of everyone. These men were here to gather unfavorable information that might punish the one they called Jim White. Apparently, this man was causing problems for the authorities. It was when the Commander was monitoring Skip Warner that he came upon a snippet of a report that involved the Princess. Suddenly the Commander became interested in Jim White. So, this man they were stalking must have had some contact with Chaldee. The Commander sat forward in his chair, searching Skip's thought processes, looking for any reference to Chaldee; immediately the name Adele White, this man's daughter, surfaced. It seemed Adele was the creator of some sort of documentary about Chaldee. The Commander was intrigued. He knew nothing of this. So, who was this child they called Adele, and how was her father so involved in this parliamentary system?

The Commander allowed himself to be propelled into the public gallery and spent the next few hours watching various members perform on this stage they called parliament. Apparently, Jim White was an independent senator, but the Commander could see that this man was not suited to the role he had taken on for he was irritated, angry, and at times ready to walk out of the chamber. Although the Commander had never seen this type of governmental theater before, it was obvious that anger was not the right tool if one wanted to be of any influence.

It was approaching lunchtime when McCloud asked if the Commander had gained any insight into how to control Jim White. The Commander was noncommittal but privately he wanted to know much more about White's connection to Chaldee.

McCloud had made arrangements to stay in Canberra until the next day, but the Commander wanted to get back to Sydney, for there was now an urgency to watch Adele White's documentary. He had begun to understand what these humans wanted from him, so if he was going to be used to attack the senator then he needed to be very sure of what he was dealing with.

McCloud was angry but eventually the Commander forced them to do as he asked. Once back in what he now referred to as his nest, hidden high among the cluster of nests, he surveyed the various boxes scattered around the room. How did they work? In what device would he find the documentary. With little success the old Commander pushed knobs and buttons on the various little sticks they called remote controls, eventually calling to the driver to come in and help. Within minutes the man had opened up a small silver container, and as his fat fingers waddled across the keyboard suddenly lights and pictures appeared on the screen.

"Can you discover where the documentary is? I know it's hidden somewhere in this box."

The driver looked uncertain. "Do you mean the thing about your alien mates?"

The Commander did not have time for anger, so he nodded emphatically.

Again, awkward fingers plodded across the keys as the driver pulled up Adele's film. "I think this's it."

"Yes … yes … it is. You can go now," the Commander said dismissively, not noticing the driver's irritation, instead turning all his attention to the screen. As he began to watch the familiar scenes of the palace, of Chaldee, of the beauty of his home, the Commander felt an aching sadness. It was not an emotion he was used to, but as he watched the devastation as the humans destroyed everything, he could feel tears forming. So, there must be conflict among these Earthlings; if somebody had created this film, then it told him that somewhere out there were humans that did not agree with such destruction. As he continued to watch, the Commander was pleased by Chaldee's haughty interaction with this man who was now manipulating him. So! McCloud had been chastised by his Princess. He smiled grimly. Much was now fitting into place. Chaldee had declared publicly who she was and the extent of her powers, and via this film he was watching it seemed Adele White was spreading information across the human world.

The Commander sat back in his chair. What did this mean? Who were the players here, and what was the endgame? Obviously, McCloud was trying to use him against his own people, and perhaps a few weeks ago when he wandered alone through what was once his kingdom, the Commander would have agreed with such a strategy, but now something felt different. He sighed dramatically. In reality he had to admit his whole viewpoint had changed. Suddenly he realized his need for revenge had disappeared. Chaldee was no longer an adversary. But what was the aim of McCloud, Warner, and the other men who came with them to watch Jim White's parliamentary performance? The information in their minds had not really told him much. They wanted Jim White to give them some sort of material—powder, they called it—they also wanted him to stop his rhetoric about their government's failure to put strategies in place for this thing called climate change. Indeed, he had picked up hints of their need for this man to die, but it was too unformed and confused to give him a complete picture.

As the Commander tried to piece together what was being asked of him, he realized he was starting to feel anxious, so he carefully took a glass over to the tap and drew out a drink. The amenities these humans had created was impressive. To build housing to such heights was clever but to bring water up here, so far from its source, really was an achievement. Thoughtfully sipping his water, he wandered over to the window. These Earthlings had developed along lines vastly different from his own people. He knew that thousands of years ago, when his people first landed on this planet their wise and honored ancestors were scientifically brilliant, but over this vast stretch of time there had been a softening, a change in attitude; there was a developing feeling of compassion and it had drawn his people toward a more mystical life journey. This was one reason why he, as a soldier, had risen up. He believed that the old ways, the ways of courage, defiance, and daring, should be restored. This was his reasoning as he tried to take control of the kingdom, and now as he watched the humans, he could see exactly the same drive. They were creative but they were also warriors, and it would seem this combination had led them to this amazing expression of life. But tears were still wet on his cheeks. He had cried when he saw his world being destroyed. These human warriors had done this—in their attitude of righteous domination—so was he with them? Or did he want to protect his race? As a soldier surely it was his duty to protect his people.

The Commander went back to his chair, staring at the blank screen. Did he need to see that film again? No! It had touched something in him that was new … perhaps even soft! Was he prepared to kill for these human soldiers? He knew his energy was still vital enough to stop a man's heart, but should he? Feeling more confused than he had ever felt before, the old soldier went across to the door. He needed the driver to take him back to the beach, where the energies were so exhilarating.

Chapter Four
Adele Comes Home

Adele waited for Jake at the airport. She knew how careful he was these days, and now that she was nursing both a bruised body and a traumatized nervous system, she understood his caution. When Jake eventually arrived, she could tell that he was shocked by her swollen face and the bruising on her neck, but as he reached out to hug her, she pulled away. "Jake, my shoulder!"

"Jeez, Adele, I'm sorry." He held her at arm's length, staring into her eyes. "You don't look well."

She nodded miserably. "I feel awful."

"Come, let's sit down … I'll get you a drink." Jake picked up her case and led her to a table. "Just sit … take a few deep breaths and I'll be back with some coffee."

"Thanks." Although she tried to smile, Adele found it hard to relax. She knew she was still angry about being attacked but whatever was happening to her now was more than just being badly beaten. The enthusiastic fire she had always felt for life seemed to have died and meeting up with Jake again made her realize just how much she had changed. Jake was still the same rough-shod defender of all things fair, but she no longer wanted to be part of it. As he hurried away, she saw him do a quick check of the area. Since he had accidently killed Martin, she knew Jake was very aware of being out in a public place, and she had always supported him, but now even his wariness irritated her. When he got back to the table, Adele tried to behave as if everything was normal. They drank in silence, then tentatively Jake asked about her shoulder.

"It's okay unless I knock it, but really, Jake, it is much better than it was."

"Right." Jake nodded rapidly. He still seemed shocked by her appearance. "And what did the police say? I guess they took statements."

"I didn't really see anything that was helpful, it was dark and pouring with rain ..." Adele paused, taking a shuddering breath. "But the thugs were wearing dark hoodies. I couldn't see them!"

Jake just nodded.

"Anyway, it's all over ... that's what Deucallus is saying."

"I only wish it was, sweetie," Jake said grimly.

"I know you think it's about the professor's material, Jake, but they were warning me. They told me to shut up and go home and I think they were trying to stop me showing the film."

"Yeah ... maybe you're right, but here there is a definite move to force our hand. They know what the professor had developed, and they are demanding we hand it over ... now they are involving your dad, too. It's a bad scene!"

"Well ... can't you just do that! I mean ... why go through all this angst, Jake?"

"That's not possible, sweetie-pie. We need to honor the old professor's legacy."

Adele took another deep sobbing breath, then shrugged. "Maybe."

"Adele, your father agrees. He knows the control they have, and he won't budge either. They cannot force us this way! What was done to you was horrific ... really ugly, and you should be angry. This is why we can't just give up."

Adele shook her head, tears rolling unheeded into her coffee cup. She saw Jake watching in dismay and knew he could not really cope with this level of stress. He always took action, he always fought back, so he would not be expecting her to collapse like this. "I'm sorry, Jake."

"Aren't you outraged? I mean … look at you! They can't do this, sweetheart!"

Half laughing through her tears, Adele reached across the table trying to calm him. "I promise I'll be outraged soon … maybe tomorrow!"

Jake smiled in relief, and they finished their coffee in silence.

"I have your father's car, and he insisted I bring you home, no argument."

Adele nodded and slipped her hand into his. Something was terribly wrong. She did not want to feel like this. She and Jake had always been together, so this sudden need to give in or turn away was almost as awful as her physical pain.

In Canberra, Jim White had become aware of being followed, but he refused to let it bother him, believing that this menace must have something to do with his very vocal protests; nevertheless, he had to admit some type of authority had him under surveillance. To add to this, Adele's shocking attack in England had affected him badly. He needed to get home to see her because he could not understand why she had been subjected to such brutality. He was angered by this constant vigil as they trailed after him each day; plus, the two henchmen were doing nothing to hide the fact that they were always there.

Now as he hurried into the airport to catch a plane back to Sydney, he again noticed the two shadows in their gray suits and conservative ties.

By the time he had arrived home he had forgotten his stalkers, for having Adele safely back was a sweet relief, although he could see she was not well. They talked a little about her time in England, and Jim was concerned by how downcast she was.

"Adele, I think you are still suffering … it was a brutal attack. Maybe you should lie down."

"I'm not sick, Dad, but you are right about me suffering. Something is not quite right here, and it makes me feel uneasy. It's as if you and Jake are creating your own drama."

"Hey, Adele, that's a bit harsh," Jake protested.

"Well, that's what it feels like. Making so much fuss in parliament that they had to kick you out! It's not helping anything, Dad!"

Jim was so shocked by Adele's accusation he could not defend himself.

"And it's so embarrassing," Suzanne White piped up in agreement. "Adele's right, Jim; you are making a fool of yourself!"

Jim did not know how to ward off this sudden attack. They obviously did not understand what he was trying to achieve, or at least his wife didn't but he had always thought he had Adele's support. After all, she was the one who had drawn him into this fight.

"I can hardly look my friends in the eye these days," Suzanne continued. "They're asking me what is wrong and why can't I manage you. It's awful!"

"Mum," Adele snapped. "Who cares what your snobby friends think!"

"Don't be rude," Suzanne complained.

Jim scratched his head, staring first at his daughter then at his wife. "What on earth are you two on about?

I'm doing what is needed to be done."

"Well, as far as I'm concerned, Jim, if you don't quit this rubbish and start behaving like a real senator, I'm giving up."

"Hey! Mrs. White, that's ..." Jake paused then turned away, and Jim realized that the younger man felt awkward challenging Adele's mother.

"I don't know why you take so much notice of those so-called friends, Mum!" Adele glared at her mother. "But my complaint is different, Dad, what I am saying is that your efforts are wasted!"

Grimly Jim jumped to his feet. "That's enough!" He stared at their angry faces, appalled by their attack.

"Adele!" Suzanne White stood up enraged by her daughter's words. "I'm not putting up with any of this." As she stamped out of the room, she added, "In fact, I'm thinking of leaving."

Adele shrugged, but Jim could see that she was shaken. "Dad, I suspect you've been an embarrassment to Mum ever since you aired my documentary."

Jim frowned in amazement.

"But ... as I say ... you irritate me for almost the opposite reasons," Adele said sadly. "You think you can solve this crisis. You think that somehow you can reverse the weather, put out the fires, fix the drought, stop the flooding, heal all illness, and prevent sea rise. Do you really believe we can overcome Nature?"

Jim shook his head as he listened. "We can do this, Adele, our ingenuity will always overcome disaster. We just need to keep trying, keep reminding people, keep giving them something to aim for."

"Rubbish, Dad."

"Hey, Adele! This is not like you," Jake protested.

"It really *is* like me, Jake; you just haven't seen me for a few months."

"We can't give up," Jim exclaimed loudly. "There is

always something more that can be done!"

"If you take a good look at the science, Dad, you'll agree. This crazy climate is being driven by predictable cyclic changes. It has very little to do with a lack of leadership or any of that nonsense! It's all happened before. It's unstoppable!"

Jim felt his anger rising. "There are always things we can do—always."

Jake looked from Adele to her father seemingly amazed by this conflict. "Jim's right, Adele. You may have been hurt or yelled at or whatever went on over there in the UK, but we cannot give up. We must offer solutions … that's the only way."

"Exactly! We must act," Jim said very loudly.

Adele was shaking her head as she listened. "Look at what we have done to this Earth, destroying forests, killing the animals, tearing great holes in the land, filling the sea with rubbish, and all for profit. We deserve what we are getting now … it's all about greed and you both know that!"

"But we can always bring about change, sweetheart." Jake hurried across, trying to hug her, but Adele moved away.

"Your reasoning is ridiculous, Adele. Do you think you would deserve to die if you were caught in a bushfire?" Jim stared angrily at his daughter. "Of course not. The bottom line is about life, Adele, life—not blame."

"No," Adele muttered, wiping away a sudden flood of tears. "It's about making a profit."

"I'm so sorry you feel like this, Adele. Maybe if you try to sleep things might look brighter tomorrow." Jim pushed aside his anger, not liking the misery he could see on his daughter's face.

For a moment Adele stood as if ready to argue, then with a slight moan, she turned away.

"Are you okay, sweetheart?" Jake asked, his face

showing the worry he was feeling.

Adele turned at the door, frowning at Jake. "No! I'm not all right and you know it; and, yes, I really do need to sleep … hopefully forever!"

As Adele limped out, Jim went to the drinks cabinet. "I need a whisky, mate! That little display was too much to handle. My wife's friends think I'm an idiot, and Adele wants me to give in. It's a lot of pressure, Jake."

Jake frowned. "I'm sure Adele will see things differently once she recovers," he said as he wandered over to the window.

"Maybe, but have you noticed … she hasn't asked me anything about how things are going down in Canberra?"

Jake frowned sympathetically.

"She used to drive me crazy with her suggestions."

"I know."

"Always trying to help because she cared … yet today she didn't even mention my bill. Something is terribly wrong, Jake."

The two men stared helplessly at each other.

"I don't know what to say, Jim, she's in a really negative place right now."

"Hmmm." Jim stared into the drink in his hand.

"Yeah … but I'm sure it'll be okay once she feels better."

"Maybe … maybe … and as if things couldn't get worse … now I'm being followed."

"Are you sure?" Jake turned, suddenly really concerned.

"I am. I've been watching them for days, and they're not trying to hide." Jim's voice faltered. "It really feels like I'm being threatened."

"But you're all right, though … nobody's …"

"No, no," Jim interjected. "Nothing like that. I just feel … uneasy."

"So, do you know how long it's been happening? I

mean, it really is a threat, Jim."

Jim felt uneasy. Obviously, Jake was concerned, which was unnerving. "It's worrying … especially if we take Adele's attack into consideration. What do you think, Jake, are the two things linked?"

Jake nodded slowly. "Maybe."

"The way I am reading it, my whole family seems to be the target," Jim said bitterly. "Adele's hurt and Suzanne doesn't seem able to cope. You've seen it; I think she even blames me for Adele's attack."

"I'm sorry." Jake seemed a little embarrassed.

"And look at Adele! She wants us to hand over the powder. It's insane … and so unlike her! We can't just meekly comply! And does Suzanne think I can just stand down because she's ashamed of me?" Jim sat down angrily. "Damn them!"

They stared at each other, indignant yet baffled.

"And this business about me being followed … do you think it's just intimidation?"

"I'm not sure, Jim. It doesn't feel right."

Jim was unable to push away his sudden fear. What had seemed to be just an odd event was suddenly becoming quite serious.

"Somehow, we need to let Paul know," Jake mused.

"How? Adele has some ability to communicate with Chaldee, but I'm not sure if she could cope right now." Jim was watching Jake at the window and he wondered just how much the younger man understood about this family upheaval. "Anyway … there's not much Paul could do." He drew a sharp breath. "Jake, you won't see anything out there now."

Jake nodded and wandered back to his chair.

"So … have you any idea what we can do about Adele?"

"Hmm … she's mad at me, too."

Jim felt sad yet mystified. He had been sure that

one day these two would marry, yet now as he felt Jake's confusion he began to doubt. There was a long, dejected silence then eventually Jim tried to change the subject. "What about Ben? When is he due to fly back?"

"I haven't heard … maybe next week."

"As soon as you see him, can you ask when he'll be going back up to the Kimberley? I think Adele should fly up with him … so she is safe."

"I agree," Jake said regretfully.

"By the way, have you shifted the powder?"

"Yes. It's in a storage facility up on the Newcastle docks … should be safe there for now but this is why we need Paul. He'll know what to do."

"And Chaldee, too. We need all the help we can get, Jake. I know we are being threatened because of the powder, but as soon as my protest starts and I get some people together, we will be stirring up another hornets' nest … or maybe poking a stick at the same hornets."

"You might be right … maybe they are the same people. It's somebody with a great deal of power," Jake mused. "But I doubt if Chaldee can do much. She is trying to create another home for her people."

Jim nodded then inched over to the window. "I know there's nobody out there … but I still feel uneasy."

"Yeah! It's a game, Jim. They're just playing on our fears."

"Well, it's working … and it's making me angry." Jim threw himself back into his chair. "You know, since Adele gave me that documentary, everything has changed for me." He paused to reflect back on his days managing the TV station. "So, I guess it's not surprising that somebody somewhere is taking notice."

"I guess so."

"And I've been doing some research. Adele's responsible for this, too; she started it! So anyway there … seems to be many questions about our planet and what influence the sun is having. I need to understand much more though if I am going to offer some sort of plan."

"Right," Jake interrupted. "Looking at stuff on the Internet might give us some idea of the cause of things like this extinction event everybody's talking about."

"Is this what we are really dealing with? Is this what they are covering up? Extinction?"

Jake sighed heavily. "I don't know, Jim. Paul has suggested it, too, but somehow the whole thing seems too awful to even consider."

"Because if it's true, not many of us could be saved. Maybe this is what Adele is talking about."

"Jeez, Jim, I don't even want to go there!"

Jim sat glumly shaking his head, unsure of the way forward. Everything had seemed ideal, even flawless when he first got involved with the documentary and Paul's people, but now Adele was telling him to quit, Jake had mentioned extinction, and somebody was obviously trying to scare him off. "So, what do we do about the professor's material, Jake? Do we give it over? Is it of any real use?"

"If Adele hadn't been hurt, I would be saying no … but there's so much more to consider, isn't there? With you being threatened and your wife wanting to leave … I just don't know, I really don't!"

Chapter Five
Death at the Town Hall Meeting

A few days after his argument with Adele, Jim was in the garden trying to appease Suzanne by replacing one of her battered rose bushes. The stormy winds of the last few days had caused such damage to some gardens that many of his neighbors were starting to build protective barriers around their favorite plants. As he tried to repair some of the wreckage, he was once again reminded that Adele, too, had been badly damaged. Remembering how her attack had both surprised and hurt him, he paused thoughtfully. He did not doubt that Adele's claim about the system being ruled by money held some truth, and in a moment of pure clarity, he admitted to himself that the massive changes needed to protect the people would not come from any parliamentary action. Although he did not like where his mind was taking him, Jim had to confess that most of the time politicians were not really in charge, which meant that his drive to become a politician in order to instigate change mimicked these pathetic garden barriers: totally useless.

Instead of being weighed down by this realization, suddenly Jim felt revitalized. Immediately he turned his attention to an idea he had discussed with Jake. They should start some type of restructuring movement. As he gently maneuvered the rose bush into place, a plan began to form. They could begin by gathering all those who already sympathized with his goals. Invite both community and commercial leadership to create a blueprint for change. Organize and promote a meeting for all those who wanted to join him. Publicly outline plans that would safeguard the population and maybe even follow that by a protest march.

Jim sat back on his heels critically examining his gardening skills. Already the rose bush seemed to have settled into its new home, and with this thought Jim admitted something else he had been trying to avoid. He, too, must find a new home if he were to honor his beliefs. By advocating a move away from the coast, he must also shift. He knew such a move would not go down well with Suzanne, so he decided that first he must find the right property, a place that might excite her. Next week he would take the car instead of flying to Canberra, that way he could spend time driving around the district in search of their new home.

To that end, he put his plans into action. He took his car to Canberra, and he drove out to Yass to look at a small farm close to the township; it was on his way back to Canberra that he began to feel uneasy. Suddenly he knew that once again he was being followed. This morning after attending the parliamentary morning session he had felt crowded, as if something threatening was close by. He had intended to explore a few more properties, but his enthusiasm faded. Jim guessed he had been upsetting a few rigid minds with his parliamentary rhetoric; surely, they would not be after him for that? So, was it this nonsense about the professor's discovery? Angrily, he admitted he had had enough. Perhaps once back in familiar territory, he would confront this intimidation, but for now he would put aside his house hunting and go home.

Within half an hour of making that decision Jim was on the road heading back to Sydney. As he drove, he tried to fix his attention on plans that would help broaden this new focus. Last week he had arranged to have lunch with an old advertising mate, Brian, who was now involved in a team designing and promoting VR games. Brian's suggestion to use this virtual reality platform as a way of presenting ideas interested Jim for it offered an entirely new yet quite radical approach to the problem of how to deal with this climatic disaster. In their conversation, Brian had mentioned the brilliant work of Ella Stone. Jim knew Ella had been a friend of Adele's at university, so as he drove, he started to formulate a few ideas that Ella might like to develop.

Jim was so lost inside his virtual reality dream that he was surprised when he realized that he had almost reached Goulburn and because he was so immersed, he had forgotten to check his rear-vision mirror. Cautiously he glanced behind, but the road looked clear. With a feeling of relief, he decided to take a break, relax with a cup of coffee, and ignore this crazy paranoia, but as he turned into a parking area suddenly the same silver Audi that had been tailing him yesterday pulled in across the road. The two gray-suited occupants did nothing to hide their interest. They sat in their car watching as Jim stood undecided. Anger burned in his gut and he was about to confront them when he saw they were leaving. So, it was just a reminder that he was still under surveillance, but for what, and why? Furiously he watched the Audi disappear. How could he put a stop to this? Somebody somewhere had the wrong information. It was obvious that there was no real threat—well, not yet anyway—so he would be best to ignore this harassment, just organize the meeting and rally. Also, he should expand on his new VR ideas with Ella Stone.

With a feeling of vigorous determination Jim drank

a cup of coffee, but as he left the café, he saw a flare of lightning sear a mass of dark clouds to the northeast. He could see that the sky had become overcast, and he knew it was foolish to ignore such stormy build-ups. These days the weather could suddenly become dangerous. Momentarily he considered waiting it out, but with such a renewed feeling of resolve he wanted to keep going. Feeling a little cautious, Jim climbed into his car. Hopefully he would miss the storm.

Jim was about twenty minutes out of Goulburn before admitting he should have waited in town. There was no way he could avoid the coming storm. Although it had not begun to rain, the wind was so fierce it was buffeting the car. The sky ahead looked black against the numerous bolts of lightning forking across the landscape. Gripping the wheel, he stared at the truck ahead; why was it slowing down? Even as this thought flashed through his mind, he heard a heavy thump, like a rock hitting the roof of his car. Then with another crash he saw something white bounce across the bonnet. It was a huge lump of hail. Jim slowed to a stop, watching as hailstones the size of golf balls began to pound the car. Now he could hardly see anything, and the noise was so loud and so terrifying he could not hear. Pulling as far off the road as possible, he tried to shelter the car under some trees, but almost immediately, he heard an explosion as the rear window smashed in. Now the storm was inside the car! As unbelievable as it was, he realized that huge hailstones were pelting the back seat. Then as the front windscreen shattered, Jim began to feel scared. For the first time in his life, he was physically exposed to the full power of Nature. As he crouched down in his seat, wet, cold, and almost senseless, he felt as if he were in a strange world.

Jim did not know how long he huddled in his car, but gradually the hammering abated as the icy balls turned to heavy rain; but the wind was still hurling water through the broken car. Jim reached for his phone. He needed help, but even as he made the call, he realized that thousands of other people would also be demanding assistance. It would be many hours before help arrived.

Shaking his head in dismay, Jim eased himself out into the rain. Now he could see many other crippled vehicles, some stranded in the middle of the road, all damaged, all victims of the storm. It looked like the scene from some disaster movie, and as he surveyed the mess, he realized that this was the kind of virtual reality game Ella could create. She could show how we live with such ease amid the solid safety of a manufactured world but in just one moment life can succumb; people can fall victim to Nature's will. Ella could make a powerful statement with images such as these.

Adele said that using a VR platform was a brilliant idea, so Jim made an appointment to see Ella Stone, persuading Adele to come with him. As the two friends renewed their acquaintance, Jim could see how this project might also lift Adele's spirits, especially as Ella was most interested in developing mini games that opened up a new way of viewing events that most people considered normal, suggesting instead that players should regard normal reality as a simulation then twisting the game into a frenzied adventure.

Ella was amused as Jim relived his experience of being attacked by giant hailstones, agreeing that it would be interesting to enlarge on this drama. As they talked, Ella began to describe a game that could highlight the inefficiency of politics then combine this with the fearsome and natural threats of Earth's climate. She said she would also include the mysteries of space, weather, meteors, and eventual extinction assuring him that the premise of this game would be the rights of citizens who were being threatened by the extremes of nature to expect protection and leadership. This would fit with Jim's warnings.

Adele listened, adding a few comments and seemingly a little more enthusiastic, but by the time they had returned home, Jim could see she had fallen back into depression. He was at a loss as to how to help, wondering if Adele should seek some type of medical advice. But as his mind went back to Ella's game, Adele's pain was pushed into the background. He knew this was wrong, and he felt guilty; nevertheless, his new drive was relentless.

A few weeks later an Indian reporter, A. J. Das, rang explaining that he knew Ella Stone well and had even helped a little with what Ella was calling Jim's Catastrophe. The reporter wanted an interview and although Jim was a little unsure, because of Ella he agreed to meet, but when A. J. began to explain he was writing a series of articles about Australian culture and that he worked for the *Times* of India, Jim felt even more dubious.

"I'm not very popular right now, so our culture is the last thing I want to discuss!"

"I know who you are, Mr. White. Many people in my country have seen the documentary you produced."

"It was my daughter who …"

"Yes, I know it was her film," A. J. Das said quickly, "but you are the one who took the risk … who put it to air. It is you my readers are interested in."

Jim nodded, still a little uncertain. "Well … ah … I guess you better sit down."

Eagerly the young Indian reporter shuffled into a seat, unpacking his laptop and adjusting his glasses.

"So, what do you really want to ask me?" Jim growled.

"Well, I would like to explore the effect that

documentary is having on yourself and the people around you … not really culture in a general sense … if you get my meaning?"

"About me personally?"

A. J. nodded. "You and your family. Could you talk a little about how you felt when you saw the amazing footage of Princess Chaldee? All this was very startling in my country. Was it a shock when you first saw your daughter's work?"

"It was. I thought it was some type of hoax to start with. My daughter was completing a university assignment, and I was sure that somehow she had created a fairy tale."

"It was an amazing scoop, being able to film this ancient race of people."

Jim nodded.

"Of course, much of what we saw in that film did not surprise my countrymen," the reporter said blithely. "Over time we have had many wise men in India who have lived extraordinary lives."

"Yogis?"

The reporter nodded enthusiastically. "Such displays of the divine arts go far back in our culture."

Jim wanted to protest, because he knew how extraordinary Chaldee was, but he was unsure of all the facts, so he simply waited for the next question.

"I believe your daughter has been showing her film overseas. Was not this a little threatening for her?"

Suddenly Jim felt uneasy. "Well … yes … she was in England."

"Were you happy about this? I mean, the film is almost revolutionary, isn't it … and she was alone."

"She had a friend helping," Jim said tightly.

"But she's home again now I believe." The young reporter seemed to be asking his questions so innocently, but Jim was now on full alert.

"Friends have informed me that she was injured," A. J. Das continued. "Who would have done this? Do you think it was because of her film?"

"This interview should not involve my family." Jim stood up abruptly. "I think you better leave."

"Sir, I am sorry if I offended you." As the young Indian was speaking, he was searching through his pockets. "But an acquaintance of yours helped arrange this meeting. He suggested I give you this." A. J. stood up, laying his business card on the desk. "I'm sorry our interview has not gone well but I will send you a copy of my article."

Without another word, the Indian reporter turned to leave.

"No!" Jim was suddenly aware of what A. J. had said. "Who helped you get in here?"

"Ah … I do not know his name, but he said he was from your office."

Jim frowned. "But who was it?"

The Indian reporter shrugged. "He did not say, he just asked me to leave my card."

"But do you genuinely work for the Indian press?"

"I do."

"Well, I'm not sure how you managed to get in here, but if you stop trying to involve my daughter, I guess you can continue with the interview. There's much I would like your readers in India to know."

The young reporter suddenly smiled. "Wonderful … thank you, Mr. White."

Jim allowed the interview to run for the next half an hour, pleased that his plans, his efforts, and maybe even his philosophy were seeping out into the wider world. When the reporter eventually left, Jim picked up the innocent business card that A. J. had dropped on the desk and saw, written on the back in red ink: "two million dollars—final offer."

Jim was deflated. The interview had gone well despite the strange way it had been organized, but now once again he was fighting this unseen enemy. They were offering huge amounts of money, they had hurt Adele, and now had used Ella and A. J. to push their case even further. They were getting inside his head, causing Jim to feel both angry and concerned. He could no longer ignore the importance of the professor's material, but just how far would they go?

Jim sat motionless for a long time. He felt there was something he was missing. What was it that was causing such blatant hostilities? He had never met Professor Egeland, but obviously the physicist was quite brilliant, and these people—whoever they were—were willing to use money and threats to get hold of his work. Jake had said something about the powder being a superconductor. What did that mean? If this material held such amazing properties, maybe it was the piece of the puzzle he was missing.

Jim flicked the card with his finger, wondering, puzzling, doubting. He really didn't have time for this problem because he had to organize his speech and get the hall ready for the public meeting he had planned, so unfortunately the hidden message given by the Indian reporter would have to wait.

Jim was pleased with the crowd that was slowly filling the hall. Because of the negativity he had been experiencing over the last few weeks, he wanted this gathering to be positive. He thought by explaining possible methods to combat the country's climate crisis, he might find more support. Australia had been facing drought, flood, and fires for so long that people were exhausted, and Jim desperately wanted them to believe there was always hope. As he busied himself with the microphone, he was reciting his opening lines. To restore people's drive, he had to offer them solutions, and a memory of a film about the second world war when Winston Churchill was able to instill this same type of courage came to mind. "We'll fight them on the beaches," he muttered as he tried to remember that famous speech. This was what was needed now for many people knew just how bad the odds were. The planet had become a very dangerous place, so it was up to him to be inspiring, to offer solutions, and to give back hope.

Adele, Ella, and quite a few of Jake's old group were helping set up the hall. It had become a happy, noisy crowd, with everybody pleased to be taking some sort of action.

Jake watched Jim, pleased that the older man seemed a little more cheerful.

"As I said, today's action will be absolutely legitimate. It's much more than a protest," Jim was explaining for the tenth time. "And I'm really hopeful that we can create a voice that will offer real planning strategies."

Jake remembered Adele's misery, and he pondered on the actual effect Jim would have on these people. As he looked for Adele, his phone buzzed. It was Ben.

"Hey! Where are you, Ben?"

"I'm at central station. My chopper's parked at a friend's farm and I came up by train, so if you give me the address, I'll catch a cab."

"We're getting ready for Jim White's protest meeting," Jake said, mouthing to Adele that it was Ben on the phone.

Adele's face lit up. "Is it Ben … is he coming here?"

Jake handed her the phone and for the next few minutes Adele almost seemed like her old self, asking Ben about his time working for a mining company; where had he left his helicopter, and most importantly, when would he be flying up to see Chaldee? Jake watched and listened, knowing that with Ben back their strength had suddenly expanded. This seemed to have occurred to Adele, too, for she had suddenly come alive.

"It's great to hear from him," Adele said as she handed back the phone.

Jake grinned, and giving Ben the address, he hung up and turned back to Adele. She smiled and for a few seconds she looked like the old Adele, so he slipped his arm around her and pulled her over to the side of the hall. "Adele, this is the first time I've seen you smile all day."

Adele tried to pull out of his grasp, but Jake's hold was firm.

"Please, Jake, don't push too hard … I just need time."

"I know that attack upset you, but it's more than that, isn't it?" Jake hesitated, pulling on his ear with frustration, not able to put his real concern into words. Adele tried to turn away, but Jake persisted. "I know something is badly wrong between us!"

Adele hesitated, staring at the floor in an effort to block him out. "I told you the other night, Jake. I told you!"

"But you were just over tired … that's all."

Suddenly Adele was sobbing so deeply he found it hard to hold her. "Nothing is as it should be." She stared into his face. "I know you understand."

Jake shook his head in helpless denial, but Adele

refused to notice.

"I feel I've changed, and it's got something to do with what Chaldee represents. Her reality … her gentle manners. Even her approach to … to … to living. It's profound." Adele pulled back and stared into Jake's face. "You can see this, can't you? Please understand."

Jake squinted at her not really grasping why she seemed so traumatized, but as she spoke, he began to realize that because of the frantic upheaval when the army tried to close Jim's TV station, and as people came out in protest, he had been too busy to notice Adele. After that, Chaldee had spent time with her, teaching the basics of telepathy, meditating with her, and talking for hours, so maybe that's when this all began.

"Please try to understand," Adele repeated tearfully.

"Hmm, I'm a bit in the dark." Jake shook his head in confusion. It seemed that she was not his Adele anymore; but because he was so pragmatic, so focused on the world around him, he could not prevent himself thinking that things would eventually be okay. So even as he gently wiped her tears away, privately Jake was deciding that Adele's so-called change was nothing more than a reaction to what had happened overseas … and in a few days she would be back to normal.

"When I was in England, I really felt excited. I had such hopes for my film because I thought the documentary would change the world. I was wrong, it just caused controversy. Some people liked it, but they treated it almost as a fairy tale, while others just baited me, yelling abuse and missing the whole point of what Chaldee represents."

"But you made an impact … you do realize this, don't you? People are changing and I am sure your film is helping." Jake smiled awkwardly.

"Look at this hall … look at the people. They all believe in Dad. They are here to support the effort he is making. They like where he is going with all this … but … but … does it really matter?" Adele sighed despondently. "Most people will not see the truth until it is too late but when I was with Chaldee something different occurred … I saw another way of doing things."

"But that's why we are all here, Adele. Your dad knows a whole new infrastructure needs to be put in place if we are going to survive. No one is talking about it, but really, I think we're at the beginning of a catastrophe … and Jim is offering alternatives."

Adele stood shaking her head as she stared around at the crowded hall. "It's not what I mean."

"What then? What do you mean?" In frustration Jake punched a fist into his other hand.

"Okay … Okay … maybe you're right … but tell me, what percentage of the population will move their homes and families or shift their business to higher ground? Who is going to start to build an alternative lifestyle?" She stared at him through tear-filled eyes. "Jake, they will not listen, not until disaster is pulling their lives apart!"

"But some people will! That's all we can hope for so I reckon you should stop saying it's too hard!"

"I'm not doing that," Adele muttered darkly.

"It can never be too late," Jake spat out angrily.

They glared at each other, aware of the chasm that was opening between them.

"I can't tell you the many times Dad has talked about the barrier reef, and what happened there around ten thousand years ago." Adele moved away from Jake as she spoke. "Of course, the reef as an ecosystem is millions of years old, but Aboriginal history remembers the current reef. The time when the water started to rise, and people had to move inland. I guess that happened at the end of the last ice age. The people back then just kept moving inland as the waters rose, but they did not have the infrastructure we have. Moving was a little easier for them, Jake, and really, we are not sure if this will happen again. I mean … this is why so many people want to deny what Dad is arguing about. They don't want him to be right!"

Even through his anger Jake could see the sadness in her eyes; instantly he realized how much he still cared for this petite, beautiful yet sorrowful person. Adele was his world, yet she suddenly seemed so remote. "I'm sorry." He tried to wrap his arms around her, but she stopped him.

"I need a little time on my own."

Jake was about to protest when he realized Jim White was mounting the platform. "We'll need to finish this later, sweet-pea, your dad's about to speak." Jake glanced around at the packed hall. "We need to get up there and support him."

Adele shrugged, but she followed as Jake pushed toward the stage.

"Good afternoon, everybody. I'm pleased to see so many of you. It helps to know we are in this together. Anyway, I'll keep my talk short so we can get out onto the street. People need to see us, listen to us, and then join us!" Jim paused, allowing a rowdy cheer to fill the hall, then he continued: "So, there are two elements to today's little speech. Fires, floods, and disease have been seriously altering our ecology and economy, so we have to encourage new ways of living together, new farming methods, innovative ways of using the land, life-changing inventions that will help protect us. This will happen because we are an inventive, creative, and forward-thinking people! This will happen because we want to continue to thrive! This will happen because we always help each other in times of crisis … and as you all know, we really are in a time of crisis. Some of our trouble is due to the blinkered, self-serving politicians who must bow before those who control the money. If we have the courage to bypass this financial domination and begin to develop a new society then our children will have a future. In the past, people like us were never considered so we must fight back if we want to save our homes and our families but now there is a general uprising across the planet. In Australia our political footprint is very faint on the road to monetary domination, so there is little we can do except become aware that these agencies have moved beyond the control of their own governments, meaning our entire planet is in a precarious place right now, so it is up to us to act, it is up to us to believe that we can bring about change, and we can! I am here today to behave like a prickly thorn warning everybody of the difficulties ahead even if we do act but warning of the suffering and death that faces us if we don't." Jim paused for a moment looking around the room. Nobody moved, so he stood in front of this silent crowd, not sure whether his words had been enough, but not willing to stand aside. He knew he was proposing a way through this crisis. They could do more than just listen, they could act! So, he stood there, waiting for some type of acknowledgment.

As he listened to the man they called Jim White, the Commander stood quietly, seemingly unnoticed by most people. Robert McCloud, Skip Warner, and two other men the Commander had not seen before crowded around him, and standing behind him, looking very menacing, was the driver.

McCloud had supplied him with a cap and very large sunglasses, so the Commander felt he was blending nicely.

The mental noise in the room was making it difficult to concentrate; nevertheless, he was able to monitor those close by, quickly realizing that the two unknowns with McCloud were high-level federal policemen; also he could feel how edgy the driver was. All five were carrying those tiny, deadly weapons, so easily hidden beneath their jackets, and as he scanned each one, he realized how opposed they were to whatever this meeting was really about.

Then the Commander turned his attention to the people on the stage, pushing his way closer in an effort to understand exactly what Jim White was trying to achieve. As he moved, the others followed closely, which made the Commander a little nervous. He was still not sure why he was here, although McCloud had warned him that Senator White, this man they thought had the powder, was a radical and what he was advocating was a plot to lure the population into unnecessary panic.

"And what would he gain?" the Commander whispered innocently, carefully monitoring everybody on stage as he listened to McCloud's mutterings.

"I really don't know what his long-range aims are, but he is certainly causing trouble with his private member's bill and you can hear what he is spouting about now … it could almost be called terrorism."

As the Commander listened, he began to recognize a similar attitude to that of Princess Chaldee. Here was another person who was fretting about the welfare of the people. It was almost the opposite to what McCloud was saying; nevertheless, the senator did annoy him, for benevolent types unsettled the people, usually by offering them visions and ideals that were impracticable.

"He's a menace," McCloud groaned.

"Try to get closer," Skip urged. "Do you have the capacity to take him out? Can you do it?"

The Commander was noncommittal. He felt sure he

had enough power to destroy Jim's life force, but did he want to? Why was McCloud so afraid? And why exert such aggression? The Commander moved against the edge of the stage watching as Jim White stood quietly in front of the people, waiting for some type of acknowledgment from the crowd. Sitting behind was his support team. Quickly, the Commander searched their thoughts, realizing immediately that the young woman was the one they called Adele, the creator of the documentary he had watched. She knew the Princess. These people were advocating a similar philosophy to that of his own people, and this struck the Commander as more than a coincidence. From being an unknown assassin, suddenly he was facing the reality of who he really was. He belonged to Princess Chaldee; he was one of her people. The Commander shuddered as he allowed these thoughts to penetrate his being, then breathing deeply he pushed aside the guilt, trying to remain focused, but as he scanned the mind of the young man sitting directly behind Jim White the Commander suddenly realized that this was the one they were looking for. He was in charge of the powder; he knew where it was! The Commander watched the young man carefully, making sure there was no mistake; but he was right, this was the mastermind McCloud was seeking, not Jim White.

The Commander turned to relay this important message to Robert McCloud but was immediately overwhelmed by a wave of violent hatred. This destructive urge radiated from the deputy secretary of the army. It seemed he had suddenly become devoured by his own need for conquest. The Commander could sense by the way the adrenalin was pounding through the man's body that McCloud wanted Jim dead. Instantly, the old fighter recognized what was at the root of this excitement. McCloud was centered on the kill. He wanted to take the senator's life, and this was exactly how he had felt during those days when he was in charge of the army. He, too, had forced his will on the people. The old Commander was both dismayed and astonished for as he saw what McCloud craved, he was forced to admit to his past, to his own murderous behavior. His automatic response came almost without thought. He had to stop this! Instantly, he sent a fatal charge of energy so powerful it ended Robert McCloud's life but as the Commander turned to focus his attention on Skip Warner, the driver saw what was happening; pushing forward he waved his gun, screaming for people to get down as he fired twice. As an accurate gunman, employed for just this type of situation, both his shots fatally wounded the Commander. Horrified by what was happening below him, Jim White launched himself off the stage, intending to intervene, but the driver mistakenly saw this as a further attack so without hesitation he fired a third shot fatally wounding Jim.

There was absolute pandemonium in the hall. The driver was instantly overpowered and as the other two police officers waved their badges and guns ineffectually, people roared in anger.

On the stage Adele and Jake saw Jim fall. Adele screamed as she tried to climb down to her father, but Jake quickly spun her around, holding her back.

"Wait, Adele, wait." Jake was trying to both hold Adele and see if Jim was moving. It did not look good. "How is he?" he yelled down to the people surrounding Jim. One man looked up, shaking his head, and Jake's heart fell. "We mustn't crowd them … they are trying to help your father," he pleaded.

"Is he okay?"

"I'm not sure. Please, sweetheart, if you will just sit, I'll find out."

Brokenhearted, Adele fell onto the chair, letting Ella comfort her.

Jake knew even before he knelt beside Jim that his friend was dead. How on earth had this happened? He looked around but beyond this bunched-up collection of saddened people he could see others around another tragedy. Crawling over, Jake peered down at the two lifeless bodies. It made no sense. Three people dead. What was happening? Jake was still on his knees, now soaked with the victims' blood, when the scream of a warning siren coming from somewhere beyond the hall immediately caused a standstill. Everybody stood motionless, caught up in the violence and the sound.

Skip Warner, who was still feeling the effects of the Commander's eyes, struggled to his feet. "Everybody … stand down." He flashed his badge. "We are taking care of this." But people were not listening. The sounds of the sirens were now passing by the hall, and at the same time people's phones began to ring with flood warnings flashing up on the screen.

"It says Sydney is flooding," somebody cried. "From some sort of tsunami or something."

"No! I don't believe it … it can't be," Skip moaned. "That crazy guy warned us!"

Jake stared at the chaos around him, the discordant phones, the warnings, and in the midst of all this lay Jim. Dead. They had actually killed him! It was madness! He struggled back up onto the stage where Adele sat rocking back and forth, moaning softly as tears streamed down her face. How could he help? Jake looked around the hall and realized that people's attention had turned away from the hideous deaths and were now pushing their way out of the hall. The warning sirens were still blasting through the whole area, and suddenly people were beginning to panic.

Jake knelt in front of Adele. "I'm sorry … I'm sorry," he breathed, his voice full of pain.

He saw Ella tentatively wanting to offer support, and he whispered, "Could you find Adele some water?"

Ben had left Jim's body and was now climbing back onto the stage. "It's a bad scene, Jake," he snapped tensely as he stroked Adele's head. "Really bad."

Jake stared down at the agitated officers surrounding the bodies. "Ben, I think we should go … we can't help Jim, and this looks really bad."

Ben nodded.

Ella was back with a glass of water, shaking and numb with shock.

"Adele, can you stand?" Jake asked gently. "We need to get you out of here, sweetheart."

"What?" Adele looked from Jake to Ben. "What do you mean?"

"What are you doing?" Ella echoed.

"This is not a good place for us to be right now." Jake vaguely waved at the milieu below. "Those guys haven't come to their senses yet, but they will … so we need to go."

"Go … but we can't! We must stay here … stay with Jim."

"Ella, Jim's gone. We can't help him now … but they'll want to interrogate Adele and they'll be looking for me, too."

"Oh!" Suddenly Ella began to understand. "I see what you are saying … but will Adele be okay?"

"We'll manage," Ben said quickly as he slipped a hand under Adele's arm, and with Ella's help they got her up.

"But … Dad! … I can't leave."

"We can't help him, Adele. I'm sorry." Ben sounded frantic.

"Their attention will soon turn to us and this is

something we don't want. We need to disappear."

"Yes … listen to them, Adele, you need to be safe," Ella said anxiously. "Your dad would have insisted."

Adele shrugged but did not have the strength to protest as Jake and Ben helped her across the stage and out the back door. The sirens were still blasting but as yet there was no hint of flooding.

"I don't know what these warnings are about," Ben puffed, "but I think we should get out of Sydney."

"Yeah … the sooner, the better," Jake agreed. "The sooner, the better, mate!"

The crisis Chaldee had forecast began with a severe earthquake in the Coral Sea just east of New Caledonia. A huge landmass beneath the ocean began to buckle causing new land to appear and the mighty waves the earthquake produced swept north, east, and west, drowning many of the islands in the South Pacific, and pushing an enormous tsunami toward the northern area of Australia. The early warning system alerted Australian authorities, but the devastation of many coastal towns from Rockhampton north to Cairns was beyond anything anyone could imagine. Townships, crops, harbors, docks were damaged or destroyed, and although not many lives were lost, the future that for many had already looked bleak, was now even worse. This unforeseen disaster added to a country already facing the effects of a climate in chaos, forcing more heartache and more devastation onto an unprepared population.

Newcastle and Sydney were far enough south to avoid the main disaster, but the predicted swell kept rising and rising with water creeping into areas that had never seen seawater before. Although there was some coordination between various authorities as they tried to deal with a population in panic, the city of Sydney was in chaos.

Dedicated supporters had stayed with Jim's body even though the sounds of sirens never stopped. As seawater seeped into the hall, they carried the three bodies onto the stage, hoping the water would not reach that far.

"It's ironic that Jim's warnings about an eventual sea rise is happening right here!" Ella muttered.

"It's not as Jim saw it, but it's certainly a taste of what might happen," someone else agreed.

Those who had supported everything that Jim stood for nodded sympathetically.

"He would not have liked this one bit," Ella mused.

They all bowed their heads in agreement, silently sitting in a circle around Jim's body. Ella had found an old stage curtain in the cupboard and they had carefully covered all three bodies with this dusty rag. Somebody else had discovered a couple of small candles tucked away in a corner, but the flickering light and the dark, sodden hall created a horror that many would never forget. The atmosphere was grim as the small gathering waited for some sort of authority to appear, but it seemed the whole city was paralyzed as the water rose and the emergency services attempted to cope with the disaster. News of the massacre at Jim White's rally was overlooked for most of the night, but as the fragile light of day touched the hall, those who stood watch stirred. Ella phoned the police again and this time she was assured that help was on its way, and within an hour ambulance, police, and the military had crowded the small car park.

Eventually Skip Warner made a reappearance, grimly surveying the terrible scene, but the culprit, the driver, the cause of the mayhem was not to be seen, nor would any person there ever catch sight of him again, for this man worked undercover, employed by Robert McCloud to take appropriate action if necessary—which he had done.

Although most of the people in the hall had to answer questions, there was no real interrogation, and even at this early stage the entire event began to sink below the awareness of most people. Warner, the man who seemed to be in charge, was anxiously pushing aside all formality. He had the bodies removed; he instructed his men to take the names of all people left in the hall; and he then ordered the place to be cleared.

Ben was frowning as they picked their way through the flooded streets. "It's madness, Jake. Everyone is knee deep in mush! What's happened?"

Jake shrugged, intent on driving.

"It looks like thousands of houses are flooded. Shops, too …"

"I don't get it," Jake muttered as he swerved to avoid an overturned rubbish bin.

"I heard a bloke saying something about a tsunami … seems a huge wave hit the Queensland coast, as far up as Cairns."

"Jeez!" Jake glanced across at Ben. "How many died?"

"I don't know. The guy said Brisbane is worse than here."

"Did you say a tsunami?" Adele murmured. "Here in Australia?"

Jake turned to look at Adele, tucked up and shivering in the back seat. She looked extremely fragile. "Just settle back, Adele, we'll take you over to your auntie Beth's." Jake spoke gently, trying to calm her, then explained to Ben: "We'll take her to her aunt's house in Penrith, she'll be safe there."

"But what's this all about, Jake? Why should Adele run?"

Jake paused as he navigated through a sheet of shallow water. "They already think Adele is part of all this."

"Yeah, well … that's just crazy … and why attack Jim? What happened back there?"

"It's such a bad scene, Ben. Somebody has been hounding Jim over the powder."

"Is that why he was shot? I mean … who are these madmen?" Ben protested.

"It's out of control, that's for sure," Jake said harshly. "The whole thing has to do with some sort of directive to confiscate the professor's work."

Ben scowled angrily.

Jake was carefully picking his way through a sodden, rubbish-strewn street. "And I think the older guy who was shot might have something to do with Chaldee. He had that look."

"Really? And what about the third man, did he have a heart attack?" Ben asked, still overwhelmed by what he had just witnessed.

"Dunno, mate!"

"Who the hell was he?"

"That's the crazy part, Ben. Who was he? I wasn't really watching, but I think it was when he fell that this whole debacle exploded."

"No wonder you want Adele out of it."

Jake took a deep breath. "She was attacked while in England … over the same thing."

"Do you think they are part of the army … you know, the ones who tried to stop the professor?" Ben frowned as he tried to straighten the muddle in his head. "I've been out west, so I know nothing about what's going on here."

"They've been hounding Jim for months, and Adele,

too." Again, Jake glanced back at Adele, who was now slumped across the seat. "She looks really bad, Ben!"

"Yeah … I can see that. Pull over and I'll drive … you try to keep her warm." Ben took off his jacket. "Here, wrap this around her," he said as he slid into the driver's seat.

Jake held Adele close, rocking her gently as Ben drove on, carefully avoiding streets that were flooded, intent on getting Adele to safety.

Slowly Adele's breathing quietened. "I think she's okay," Jake muttered. "I hope so. I'm not good at this kinda stuff."

Ben smiled a little at this pathetic confession.

"So, when we get Adele to safety then I want to check on the powder … see if it's still there. I'll bet Newcastle is just as badly flooded as here."

"Is that where it is?"

"Yeah … on the Newcastle docks!"

"Oh, mate, no! That's sure to be flooded!"

"I know, I know … but who would have predicted a tsunami? Anyway, I'll go up and check it out, you head back to the farm and wait down there. Hopefully they will hold Jim's funeral quickly."

"I doubt that … not if what you say is right. They'll delay the whole thing for weeks."

Jake nodded, still holding tightly to Adele. "I guess so." He paused as he tried to form their next move. "If you wait down there, we'll eventually get to you … then we'll fly up to Chaldee."

Adele raised her head and looked at Jake. "Did you say Chaldee?"

Jake nodded.

"We'll get you up there soon, Adele," Ben tried to sound cheerful.

"Yes," Jake agreed. "The sooner we get out of this place, the safer it will be for all of us."

Adele nodded and lay back against Jake. “Please let it be soon,” she whispered.

Part Three
Stepping into Another World

Chapter One
Reunion in the Underground City

As the familiar sound of a helicopter filled the caves, every person came to an abrupt halt, tension gripping their hearts. Were the human soldiers back? Then slowly, as the droning whine moved above the cave, they realized that the craft was flying up to Ben's hidden landing field.

"It's Ben! I think it's Ben!" the Master Speaker said excitedly, rushing to the cave entrance. Others crowded behind and within a few minutes they heard Ben calling a greeting.

"Ben, we are here." The Master Speaker slid back the covering and the happy crowd pushed their way out, shouting a welcome as they watched the Earthling pilot climb down the rocky incline, turning to help Adele, who seemed very weak; then they saw a new face.

"This is Jake everybody," Ben said giving a quick introduction. "He's a friend of Paul's."

"You are all welcome … welcome. Indeed, you are such a wonderful sight … we are beyond happiness." Zell was stumbling over his words his excitement was so great. "Please come … come … you must be tired." The Master Speaker led the way inside unaware of the intense look Jake was giving him.

Ben also saw this strange look on Jake's face. It seemed almost as if Jake recognized the old man. He hesitated but then decided to ignore it. "It's been a bit of a trip. Took us much longer this time as some of my old stopovers are gone. It's this drought … it's forcing people to leave the bush," Ben explained as he moved into the cool shade of the cavern. "And Adele is not well … she needs to lie down."

All attention turned to Adele, and within minutes they had helped her into an old rocking chair, surrounding her with comfortable cushions and rugs.

"Thank you," she whispered, laying back wearily. "Is Chaldee here?"

"No, Miss Adele, … but I will explain later. Now you must have drinks and food." Zell gave a few quick commands and soon the three were eating their first real meal in quite a few days.

"So, where's Paul and Chaldee?" Ben eventually asked.

"Ah … they are searching for our new home." The Master Speaker nodded toward the back of the cave. "Paul felt there might be something special farther in."

"That sounds like Paul," Jake said tersely.

"Any idea when they'll be back?"

The Master Speaker drew a deep breath knowing his news would be upsetting. "I'm afraid there has been an accident. Paul slipped while exploring an unknown area."

Both Ben and Jake looked startled, then anxiously Jake scrambled to his feet. "Where is he now … how bad is it?"

"Please … try to remain calm. Chaldee is with him," the Master Speaker said gently. "I have much more I must explain … things you might find hard to believe."

"Nothing up here surprises me." Ben smiled slightly as he pulled Jake back into his seat.

"Yes, I am trying to view our world from your eyes,

Ben, but it is difficult. I beg for your attention as I try to explain." The Master Speaker paused, trying to put his thoughts in order. "Princess Chaldee had a visitation from a Being who brought her the news of Paul's accident. This Being … ah … this entity … well, he simply appeared in front of her."

"Something like the Oracle? He's another entity who just appears from nowhere," Ben said. "I remember when I first saw him … here in these caves actually."

The Master Speaker nodded. "Perhaps! You could draw a likeness I suppose, but this Being says he is from an inner-Earth city, only a few hours from here."

"Inner Earth?" Jake was on his feet again. "Do you mean underground?"

The Master Speaker nodded.

"Jake, the world we are in here … it's not quite the same as being in Sydney." Ben stumbled over his words as he tried to explain. "I know it takes some getting used to, but you'll just have to accept what the Master Speaker is saying."

"This Being told the Princess that they have taken Paul to a healing facility in their city. Princess Chaldee and Joe are with him now."

"Have you any news?" Jake demanded. "How is he hurt?"

"His back and leg are damaged, and when the Princess contacted me, she said they were using some of the professor's powder. Apparently, it has had quite a powerful effect." The Master Speaker paused as he saw Jake's horrified expression.

"I realize how important this material is," Jake whispered. "But there has been … ah … a huge accident. How much do you have left?"

"Although we sent a great deal down with Ben last time he was here, Aegeus has been very busy. He is quite brilliant, so our stocks have been replenished."

"Jeez … that's good news because some really bad stuff has happened to us, too, over the last weeks. The area where the stocks were stored was flooded … and all the powder was destroyed, I'm afraid."

"Destroyed?" the Master Speaker repeated in shock.

"Yeah … We had a huge tidal wave … a tsunami. It washed away the entire storage area on the docks … I'm sorry … I had no idea such a thing could happen."

"I think I understand." The Master Speaker could see Jake's distress. "Princess Chaldee was warned of this catastrophe, so please do not be upset … apparently your authorities did nothing."

"Can we talk about that in a minute, Jake?" Ben cut in as he looked across to where Adele was sleeping. "Maybe the powder could help Adele, too. She's still in shock. So tell us about Paul … how are they using the powder with him?"

"I am not sure, Master Ben."

"A mate told me how important this stuff is," Jake muttered in a dull voice. "So, it'll probably help her."

"It is quite miraculous." The Master Speaker turned to Shorna. "Mix a little powder in some water. When she awakes, you could try to give Adele a small sip. It may help."

Shorna nodded and hurried away.

"And what about Paul?" Ben said.

"Yeah … yeah … could we go to wherever he is? I'd like to be with him," Jake said miserably.

"Of course, I shall ask the Princess immediately." The Master Speaker moved into the shadows, as he telepathically tried to make contact with Chaldee.

Ben and Jake were on edge as they waited, then Jake whispered: "That weird guy at Jim's meeting … the one that was shot … don't you think he looks a bit like the Master Speaker?"

Ben frowned as he tried to remember.

"When I saw him, I thought something looked familiar."

"Maybe."

"Maybe what?" Adele said sleepily as she wriggled out from under all the blankets.

"Let's talk about it later, we've just asked if we could try to get to see Paul."

"Oh!" Adele looked stressed. "Jake! I don't think I can make it … not if I have to do any climbing."

"No … no … you just stay put. They'll look after you here. Don't even think about trying to move."

Adele settled into her chair; weariness etched across her face as she drifted back to sleep.

"She's a mess," Ben said sadly. "I hope the powder helps."

"Yeah … maybe it will, though losing her father like this is a huge trauma, and I don't seem to be of any help anymore … add this to the battering she took in England … it must be like some type of inner bombshell!"

Ben nodded and there was a thoughtful silence as they waited for the Master Speaker to return.

Chaldee was walking across a wide, polished concourse when she realized the Master Speaker was trying to contact her.

"Yes, Zell, what is it?"

"Master Ben, Adele, and another man they call Jake have just arrived, and they want to see Paul."

"Oh, that's marvelous!" Chaldee was surprised but also pleased. "I am sure Paul would be glad to see them. He is not yet able to sit up, but his wounds are healing. The powder is quite miraculous."

"I remember back to when you were badly injured. Aegeus used the powder then, and you healed very quickly."

"Indeed, I did, Zell!"

"Adele seems unwell and we intend to give her a little of the powder."

"Oh, I'm sorry. You must not allow her to come, Zell, not if she is feeling ill. The rough terrain would be too difficult."

"Of course, Madam. So, I will tell them to join you."

"I will arrange for somebody to meet them at the gateway. It is hidden so they will have to be guided in."

"Very good … I will explain and will set them up with the necessary equipment."

As the Master Speaker receded, Chaldee turned back to the healing center. She knew Paul would be glad to see his friends so hurriedly she ran down a shallow set of stairs and onto another concourse. The entire city appeared to be formed out of cut stone, with smooth, polished walls that shone with the sparkle of natural quartz. The wide corridor-like streets were immaculate and curved around a series of flat open areas that were built on many levels. Chaldee had only seen this tiny part of the city, but she could tell it was quite large, and from what she had seen, almost empty. She had no idea how many people lived here, and knowing how often these beings spiraled out of body she realized there could be thousands of people here; nevertheless, the few who glided past were of the same tall, opaque, glimmering appearance as Isaak and Abe.

When she reached the healing center, Chaldee could see that Paul was now sitting up. Excitedly she skipped across to his couch. "You are doing so well!" She kissed him lightly. "I am beyond relief!"

"I feel great."

"The Master Speaker has just made contact. He said

that Jake and Ben have arrived at the cave and want to see you."

"Why are they up here?" Paul asked dubiously.

"I don't know but they will be with you soon enough … so you can ask them."

"Where are Adele and Jim?"

"Adele is also here, but she seems a little unwell, which is worrying. Zell said nothing about Mr. White."

"Okay." Paul lay back, his face suddenly clouded. "I feel something is wrong."

Chaldee sat beside the bed and took his hand. "You must not allow negative thoughts to interfere. You are doing so well."

Paul nodded, silently gripping her hand.

As she read his thoughts, Chaldee realized that he was still a little unstable. The fall had injured more than his body; his nervous system was tight, edgy, and fearful. She leaned across the bed and drew him to her. "You need to rest." She felt his trembling weight and she wished she could do more than just hold him. He had lost so much strength yet when she counted back to the time of his fall it was only two days ago. "You are doing so well, and sleep will help enormously." Tenderly Chaldee lay him back on the pillows.

Paul nodded again, his eyelids flickering closed.

"We will wake you when Ben and Jake arrive."

Chaldee crept out of the room and at the door she was met by another being, a very tall, shining female, who spoke softly as she introduced herself: "I am Asher, Abe's wife." Then to Chaldee's great surprise the stranger leaned forward and kissed the Princess on the cheek. This was the first time any stranger had ever addressed her in this way and Chaldee was uncertain as to how she felt. It was an effrontery but at the same time she felt a warmth coming from Asher.

"I am Chaldee."

"Princess Chaldee," Asher corrected softly.

"Yes." Chaldee smiled, suddenly realizing that here was another being who would become a friend.

"Abe has suggested that we gather in the great hall to welcome you."

Chaldee stepped back in amazement.

"Yes, my dear, we are well aware of who you are, and have been watching ever since the Earthlings destroyed your palace." Asher took her hand. "Please, if you will come with me, there are people eager to meet you."

Chaldee followed, still slightly perplexed. Obviously, these strange light-beings were highly skilled in the movement across dimensions. Their tall, painfully thin bodies hardly seemed to exist in this realm, yet this marvelous city was proof that they knew how to manipulate matter.

After walking up many of the wide shallow staircases and across what felt to be acres of beautifully decorated concourses, they eventually reached the building Asher referred to as the great hall. It was very large, with a ceiling so high Chaldee could only just see the outline. There was also a gentle blue light that seemed to glow from the walls, turning the great room into a breathless shade of turquoise.

Pushing through the heavy doors, Chaldee was met with the instant sound of clapping. There were certainly many people here to welcome her, all of them translucent. Asher led her to the dais where Isaak and two other very tall beings were waiting to greet her. Again, there was clapping as Chaldee mounted the steps. Graciously she offered her hand to each of them.

"Welcome, Princess Chaldee, we are pleased to talk with you."

Chaldee took a regal position on an empty chair, staring out across the hall. The sight of so many shimmering entities created a misty light that combined beautifully with the blue glow of the hall.

"We will not keep you long, Madame, but it is so rare for us to have such an honored guest, there was a universal demand that people be allowed to meet you."

"I, too, am honored," Chaldee said hesitantly. "It has been long since I have been celebrated in this way. As you all must know my kingdom has been destroyed so these days our day-to-day existence is precarious."

"We are aware of your circumstances, My Lady, and are eager to offer help if this is acceptable."

There was another burst of clapping, and suddenly Chaldee felt overcome. Since her kingdom had been destroyed, she had borne the burden of her people's distress, now these strangers were opening their hearts to her. She stood up, wiping away her tears. "I am overwhelmed by your generosity and your compassion. I thank you all." She bowed slightly, then sat down amid more enthusiastic cheering.

As the hall slowly began to empty, some beings came up and offered their hand or gently touched her. Chaldee turned to Isaak: "I cannot believe the generosity of your people, sir. I thank you again."

Isaak leaned down and he, too, kissed her cheek. "You are most welcome. People want you to realize that we know who you are and that you are in their thoughts. We were devastated when we saw what was happening to your palace."

Chaldee nodded. "The Earthling army has much to answer for."

Isaak frowned but did not speak.

"But … as you have seen yourself, I have the friendship of other wonderful Earthlings who are here with me now, so please believe me when I say not all humans are barbaric."

Isaak's smile was rueful: "We, too, are human, Princess Chaldee, so I am indeed aware that we are not all barbaric … but our personal history is different to the current day. The circumstances that brought our ancestors here can be thought of as uplifting. I will relate our history later if you are interested, but right now I feel you should get back to Paul."

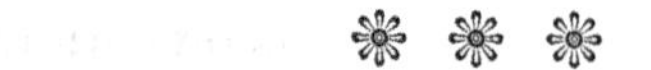

In the caves Ben and Jake were preparing to leave. Joe had sent a message that he and Abe would head out and meet them somewhere along the tunnel system. Eventually the Master Speaker sent through another message saying the boys were on their way, and for the next few hours Ben and Jake forged through the same narrow, rough, rocky darkness as Joe and Paul had faced. Neither said very much as they followed the narrow light beams from their helmets.

Eventually Jake complained. "Jeez … this is painful … no wonder Paul fell."

"It's a bit of a challenge," Ben puffed. As a pilot Ben found little reason to walk, meaning he was so unfit that this shadowy passageway was pushing him to his limit. They reached the narrow ledge that seemed to be a rim around a deep chasm and for a moment they were not sure which way to go, so they shed their packs and sat down in the darkness. Then as they heard a yell from farther down the tunnel Jake relaxed, leaning back against the gritty wall. "I've never been so happy to hear Joe's voice," he said, amused at his own pathetic feeling of relief.

"Hey, you guys, welcome to our new world," Joe yelled as he caught sight of them.

There was a lot of backslapping as the three friends joyfully said hello; even so, Jake was aware that Abe stood aside watching this melee waiting to be introduced, and he realized what the Master Speaker was referring to when he had said they were in for a shock. Abe was the tallest being Jake had ever met, yet he was almost too thin to exist, and his large head seemed not to fit his body.

"This is Abe, he'll show us the way but be careful, this is the area where the cave wall gave way and Paul fell," Joe warned.

Jake nodded hello and was surprised when Abe replied: "I can see that you are very close to your friend, you must not fear for him."

Not able to cope with the type of emotion implied by Abe's words, Jake asked awkwardly: "How is he?"

"Well … let's say he is better than anyone expected," Joe answered. "When I got to him about ten minutes after he crashed onto the ledge, I didn't think he had a hope." Joe shook his head as he remembered. "It was terrible. His leg was broken, and he had a head wounds that bled so badly I could not stop it … and then I realized his back might be broken too, yet two days later, and he's almost healed. These guys," Joe waved at Abe, "these guys are fantastic."

Jake stared at Abe, trying to unravel his confusion. "Thanks!"

Abe smiled. "Let's go, I hate this miserable place."

They all nodded in agreement, and within another hour they had left the tunnel and were walking down the wide, highly polished entrance to the city. Ben felt it was almost like a dream, and Jake wondered how such a magnificent place could exist so far beneath the surface; then as Abe began to reply Jake realized this stranger was aware of what he was thinking. So, here was someone else who could mentally tap into thought patterns. He felt so uneasy that he missed what was being said.

"… and we eventually started …" Abe was speaking but Jake spluttered across his words.

"Sorry … sorry, Abe, … I missed what you said."

Abe slowed down and turned to Jake. "Do not apologize for I know how confused you are."

Jake just nodded.

"I was explaining that originally our First People tried to build a city farther down along the cave system, in some very large caverns that still had a source of light, but every year, in the wet season, the tiny stream that trickled through their village became a huge river and their homes were regularly flooded, so eventually my forefathers moved their dwelling to this place. I guess one could say my people have always been here … although this city is even older than we are! It seems nobody knows who the builders were. There is a fissure in the Earth, high above the roof in the top area of the city. This gives us a tiny opening to the world outside, and we have miles of exhaust pipes bringing air in."

"And the lighting?" Ben asked. "How does this work?"

"We use a crystal power system."

"Wow!" Suddenly Jake understood. "So … are you guys Atlanteans?"

Abe paused, then said very slowly: "We are not, although our ancestors became part of the Atlantean system. It is very complicated because our origin reaches back into Lemurian times, but we lived alongside the Atlanteans. My people moved here over eleven thousand years ago … they sought refuge here during the final days of that period, but we have advanced far beyond who we were back then." Abe paused, glancing from Jake to Ben as he tried to explain. "Our race is different from the civilization you are calling Atlantis, yet we are all human."

"But … you do know about Atlantis," Ben said excitedly. "Is that why this place is so perfect?"

Jake grinned. "Just amazing."

"And it's huge," Joe added.

Abe smiled gently. "Although it is our home, this

place is much older than we are … but thank you … it is not often that we entertain outsiders, so it is nice to see my home through your eyes."

Again, Jake realized his thoughts were being monitored, but this time he did not mind. Suddenly he felt a level of enthusiasm and excitement that he had not felt for a long time.

Moving farther along the wide polished corridor, Jake, Ben, and Joe were almost speechless as they tried to absorb the city's uniqueness.

Eventually they passed under a high archway. "We are here," Abe announced. "And I believe that Princess Chaldee is with Paul, so we can go straight to the recovery rooms."

Paul was laying back in a large, comfortable lounge chair when the group walked in. As the two friends saw each other, a powerful reunion took place. Neither Jake nor Paul had realized just how much they had missed each other. Paul kept shaking his head, unable to comprehend that it was Jake in front of him. "How'd you get here, mate? When? How?"

Jake laughed as he grabbed hold of Paul's hand. "It's good to see you sitting up! They said you were recovering but this is terrific!"

Both laughed as Jake bent over and hugged his friend.

"We flew in early this morning," Ben explained.

"Abe came with me and we met them halfway down the tunnel," Joe added.

"… and came straight here … although when we first arrived at the caves, I had no idea you were hurt,"

Jake continued.

Chaldee moved across to Jake extending her hand. "I remember you from Sydney. You stayed behind with Deucallus and Adele." Chaldee frowned. "And I heard she is not well?"

"She's really upset … sadly we have some bad news … but let's leave it for now. It's so good to be here," Jake said carefully, not wanting to dampen the atmosphere.

"I'm blown away … having you all here … It's great, isn't it, Chaldee?" Paul lay back exhausted but smiling.

"There are others here, too," Chaldee explained. "Aegeus, my amazing young scientist, and Joe's offsider, Enka, they have gone with Patch, out exploring the city."

"We have decided we must have a celebratory meal here in Paul's room, so they may be helping with preparations," Abe said softly. "We do not eat often, as we have little need of food, but on this occasion we will indulge."

"And it is an occasion, is it not? We represent three different cultures," Chaldee said thoughtfully. "I think it might be historic!"

As she spoke, dishes of food arrived and tables and chairs were brought in.

"Before we eat, let me send my appreciation to all who are not here. We are one." Isaak briefly lowered his head, then looked around at all his guests. "It is a joy to be here with you all."

Soon the whole group had gathered around Paul and were eating delicate finger food.

When Isaak gave his brief salute, Paul had felt its power. These new feelings were becoming common, and Paul, although pleased, was mystified by the energies he was now feeling. He wondered if the powder used to help his healing was contributing to these waves of awareness radiating through him. He looked across at Chaldee as she chatted lightly with Ben. Even Chaldee's energy felt delightful. He took a deep breath, not quite knowing what was happening but hoping these feelings would become permanent. He lay back in his chair, feeling tired, not really listening to the conversation but feeling more content than he had felt for many years. The old agitation as his mind jerked from one thought to another seemed to have eased. There was a quietness within that felt wonderful.

Chaldee smiled and he nodded, knowing that she was feeling this change in his energy pattern. Jake also kept glancing across at Paul. Maybe he, too, felt the difference.

As Paul lay back watching the life flow of all these people, he realized that Jake and Joe were busily catching up. Immediately he remembered how much had to be done if he was to find Chaldee somewhere to live. Momentarily he felt anxious, then the feeling faded. There was time. There would always be time.

"You are right, Paul," Abe said. "You do have time! Also, you can look to us for help. I am sure Isaak will speak about this soon."

Paul stared up at Abe. "You read my mind?"

Abe nodded.

"Hopefully soon I will also be able to do this." Even as he spoke, Paul was amazed at himself. Chaldee had been in his head from the first moment they had met, and it had always angered him. Now suddenly he realized that this was the most genuine, purest way of relating. No lies or hidden meanings, just total truth.

Abe smiled and touched his hand. "I am actually witnessing your expansion, Paul. It is quite amazing."

Paul cocked his head on one side as if asking a question though he did not speak.

"There is much we can discuss if you feel ready."

"I'm aware of some sort of huge inner change. I suspect it has something to do with my fall … maybe when I hit my head?"

"Maybe, but the powder's influence is part of your new awareness. It creates a quickening of the mind's patterns." Abe paused, then said softly: "Your professor was a brilliant man. He has produced a material that will assist with the changes that are about to transform your people. This powder has qualities that can assist the awareness of the heart."

"What do you mean, Abe? Remember it's me you're talking to … and up until a few days ago I would not have even considered stuff like this!"

"But you are involved with Chaldee? Surely you realize how she used her power. It comes from the heart."

Paul smiled, showing his embarrassment. "This has been a huge problem for me because up until a few days ago I wasn't able to even contemplate the idea of energy fields or levels of awareness."

Abe stared at Paul. "Perhaps it was fear that was blocking you."

"Absolutely! The whole thing scared me, because I have always liked to know that the world around me is rock solid … that reality is set in concrete … that things are just as they seem. Do you understand?"

"I do."

"But now for some reason I'm not so threatened by the idea that reality's an assimilation of some kind."

There was a small silence as Paul and Abe considered the meaning behind Paul's confession.

"So perhaps I could offer you a little more information. Details that need great contemplation," Abe said hesitantly.

Paul drew a sharp breath.

"It seems you are able to consider that reality is actually a projection. Thought creates this realm, Paul. Collectively we maintain this world. If one were poetic, one could describe it as light flowing through geometric patterns in the field of consciousness … or maybe not."

Abe laughed lightly.

Paul shook his head slowly. "I have read about this stuff but until now it has never made any sense."

"And now it does?" Abe seemed pleased.

"Well … sort of."

"So, let us travel a little deeper. What if I suggested that you are not your body, that you are broadcasting your thoughts from a state of consciousness beyond the realm of matter?"

Now Paul was adamantly shaking his head. "You can't possibly be serious?"

Abe beamed. "But I am, and you know I am, and you also know this is how things really are … but just wait, Paul … think about it; consider this as you muddle through. All your thoughts are directed toward your physical body; a body that feels joy or pain and you are the one operating this robotic instrument; you are broadcasting into the body and you gain from every experience. This is what life here in this dimension is all about. The experience."

As Paul listened, he was scratching his head. "Sorry, Abe, too much information."

"But it's in there now, and you will think about it, I know."

"Me no can compute." Paul laughed.

"What can't you compute?" Jake asked as he moved over to stand beside Paul.

"Mad stuff, mate, stuff that's beyond me … beyond you, too, I suspect."

Just then Isaak stood up, tapping his glass. "People, can I have your attention?" Isaak said quietly.

Paul watched thoughtfully as Isaak glanced around at the large group. "What I am seeing here today is unprecedented. To have such a mixture of tribes yet to be so harmonious fills me with hope."

Eagerly Paul balled his fist, punching the air. "I agree."

Isaak smiled as he acknowledged Paul's leadership. "Paul is recovering well, and much thanks must be given to the powder your people have produced. Such magical energy is something we could benefit from, too."

"Aegeus will share his knowledge with you. He has much to offer." Chaldee glanced at Aegeus, who looked away in embarrassment.

"Yes, I realize that Professor Egeland wanted to share the power of this material with the world." Isaak paused as they all nodded in agreement, then he looked across at Jake. "But I fear something quite terrible has happened. Could you tell us, Jake?"

Miserably Jake nodded. "I didn't want to dampen people's spirits, but apparently some of you have already picked up certain facts."

"What's happened?" Paul was suddenly concerned.

"Please ... can we leave this till later?"

"No, we must hear it in your own words, Jake," Chaldee said sadly.

Paul could see that whatever had happened had drained Jake's fire. His inner ability to use a practical approach to fix all problems seemed to have left him. "Tell us."

"Jim White is dead. He was shot by some secret-service madman."

"No!" Paul fell back in his chair.

Ben dropped his face into his hands, and Paul guessed it was because the pilot was remembering the dreadful scene.

"That's what Adele is trying to cope with," Joe muttered.

Paul realized that Chaldee knew what Ben and Jake had witnessed, this was why she was so sad as she watched their reaction.

"How is such a thing possible?" Isaak was reacting to their distress. "What do you mean—shot?"

Paul scratched his forehead as he looked across at Isaak. "We live in a brutal world. This man, Jim White, was an activist. He was trying to put plans into place that would give people hope, offering ways to cope with the climate catastrophe that threatens us."

"Yet, you say he is dead … that someone killed him! How could this happen?"

"As Paul says, there is an element of brutality in human society," Chaldee said quietly.

Ben seemed shocked, but Jake nodded in slow agreement.

Paul shrugged helplessly. "I can see how an outsider might see us."

"Not you, Paul. Not the people here … no! We know human society is complex. Some Earthlings are aggressive killers while others are almost divine," Chaldee explained. "But the key problem is that humans believe they are separate from each other when really they are not!"

"It's the way it has always been. This is how all Earthling civilizations function, My Lady." Isaak frowned. "It is very hard to explain."

"Maybe … but I think I might understand," Joe said thoughtfully. "Because when Isaak says there are three tribes here today, that really is not correct. There are four. My people have lived on this land for over eighty thousand years … and our love of the land is spiritual, this is why we are different."

Isaak nodded toward Joe.

"This is why living with Chaldee's people is such a blessing."

"Was it that bad, Joe?"

"I think it is the same for all people, Joe," Isaak said calmly. "The human need for power has always been a driving force on this planet. What I am about to say may seem a little bizarre but it's the way we humans grow … through experience."

"I am not sure if I understand," Jake said doubtfully. "Do you think that regardless of positive or negative attitudes, we still develop?"

Isaak nodded. "Yes. A person may experience the most horrific circumstances, nevertheless their ability to deal with whatever they face sometimes triggers amazing growth. My own people have certainly developed over the long period we have been living in this reality. Also, our storytellers tell how the Atlanteans were both destructive and creative, very similar to this present human civilization."

"As I was saying, Isaak, it is quite a cruel world," Jake muttered. "And Adele is feeling terrible right now."

Joe grimaced. "This is shocking!"

"Adele is heartbroken."

"And has anybody been arrested?"

"No, I'm afraid not, but there is much more." Jake stood up and wandered away from the group.

Paul watched his friend carefully. He could see how disturbed Jake was.

Ben reached out to support Jake, then turned back, explaining: "It was chaotic. There was a guy there who looked a little like the Master Speaker … he was shot first, then Jim tried to intervene, but the same idiot shot him. The whole thing took less than a minute, but at the end of it, three people died."

"Oh dear … I am starting to understand," Chaldee whispered. "The Earthling soldiers captured one of our outcasts, the Commander. I knew he was down there with that government man."

"You mean McCloud?" Jake asked.

"Yes, that's right, but there were others, too. They were trying to get the Commander to mentally assess Mr. White because they believe he had the powder … but from what you are saying, the Commander did not act as he was supposed to, though I have no idea how he could have killed someone … we are not allowed to use our energy that way!"

"Well, I think he did," Jake muttered.

"This is beyond belief, guys!" Paul lay back staring up at the very high ceiling.

"And so, Jim dies, but nothing is done. No investigation, no police report, no arrests," Jake said angrily.

"You said it was at some sort of rally Jim had organized? Surely someone has said something." Paul was completely puzzled. "It can't all just disappear! This is murder!"

Jake scratched his head as he replied: "It was really chaotic because of the tsunami."

"What about Jim's body?"

"Apparently, Suzanne—his wife—got a message saying that Jim had died of a heart attack. That's about all I know because we just ran."

"They'll be looking for you," Paul said with concern.

"That's why we're here."

"Wow! I can't take it all in." Paul lay back in his chair. "You say there was a tsunami?"

"Up north. It came in from the Coral Sea … but I haven't read many reports."

"This is all quite terrible, Paul, but I think you should try to rest," Chaldee said quietly.

"Yes, you are right," Isaak said, nodding his head. "He needs to rest."

"I'll stay with him." Jake sounded so determined nobody argued and slowly they tidied the room and by the time they had left Paul already appeared to be asleep.

Chapter Two
Planning an Attack

A small crowd pushed into Skip Warner's office, officers whom Warner had handpicked for a special operation and who were now listening intently, trying to grasp the importance of what he was saying.

"I know the whole thing sounds impossible, but this old guy was able to pick up stuff I was thinking. He was reading my mind! Rob McCloud knew him, knew how to use him, but then something went wrong!"

"Can you explain how, sir?"

"I can't give you a full account," Skip said solidly, staring round at this group of puzzled officers. "Seems the old man turned on McCloud … why I don't know." He shrugged, then turned back to the blackboard.

"How did Mr. McCloud die, sir?"

Skip Warner paused, playing with the drama of the moment, before answering softly: "It has to remain secret." He let the silence in the room deepen, for he knew Rob McCloud's death hung there, almost as a threat, which would certainly make these men more cautious. Eventually he continued. "So … people … this is what we have right now; intel reporting that when Professor Egeland produced a material that our boffins say has important properties, it was given to a senator … Jimmy White. You may have heard of him. He was making all sorts of fuss about the climate."

There were a few groans and nods.

"Anyway, White had control of this powder but unfortunately, he died, so we can dismiss his involvement, but there are others out there who know where the stuff is, and I have orders from the top—I repeat … from the top—ordering us to retrieve all this material. It is too valuable, too technologically sensitive to have civilians charging about with it, so we must detain these people and recover the material." Skip Warner looked around the room, noting how intense the atmosphere had become. "Let me emphasize … this is of vital importance! We must recover both the powder and the professor's papers as soon as possible."

"From my information this is a mess your people have not been able to sort out, Warner." The officer who spoke sounded sarcastic. "There have been too many deaths, too many mistakes. I know you have just taken over, but everybody here must be told all the facts."

Skip Warner stared bitterly at the speaker. "Yes, we know that, but just let me run this thing as I see fit. You give me information and I'll use it. More in-depth data is what I need to put this whole thing together."

The two senior officers glared at each other. Skip was head of the strike team, but Michael Taft was a technical officer supplying background checks and all supportive information. He knew the complete history of the professor and he had data on the amazing documentary produced by Jimmy White and his daughter Adele. He felt that Warner and his team really did not understand the subtleties of this investigation, so he was determined to make this briefing as thorough as possible.

"We have managed to keep the deaths under wraps," Skip continued. "Well … for now anyway, thanks mainly to the tsunami." Skip paused to look around at his team. "We had a stroke of luck for a change. The entire country is focused on the devastation in Queensland. Nobody is showing any interest in what happened at White's rally."

The men listening nodded cautiously. Even Taft did not argue.

"So, we have managed to 'disappear' McCloud's body for now. In a few weeks his death from a brain aneurysm while overseas will be announced. He doesn't have any close family, so hopefully we'll get away with it. Jim White's body has been returned to his family. They were told he suffered complications from a stroke, and I believe he has already been cremated … is that right, Michael?"

"Yes. His wife did not make any sort of fuss. She seemed very withdrawn; in fact, I suggest she is too frightened to ask questions. Maybe she has some idea of what happened to her husband, but she'll not make trouble."

"Yeah … I heard that. Her behavior is a bit strange," Skip said hurriedly, as if wanting to bypass any unseen difficulties. "But his daughter Adele was not at the funeral. She seems to have disappeared, and this is why you guys are all here. Adele White is a person of interest. She must be found. We are sure she knows the whereabouts of the powder."

"But his wife … would she know something?"

Skip shook his head. "No, she's too scared and too vague. We talked to her, but it was easy to see she is not in the loop. No! It's the daughter … that's who we must find. She helped make that documentary and has recently returned from a publicity tour in the UK. Adele White is who we need to speak to."

"What about her boyfriend?" Taft reminded Skip. "We haven't anything on him. Not much history at all. Apparently, they met at secondary college … so is he just the boyfriend?"

"I'm not sure about him. What's his name?"

Michael Taft checked his notes. "He doesn't appear anywhere although there's a brief report from Roccia that mentioned a Jake Anderson."

"Probably the same guy, but really it is Adele White we are searching for. So that's the first point, but I think what's more important is to take our search up into the Kimberley area. The old codger we were working with … the Commander … was found wandering around up there in the destruction area."

"Destruction, sir, … should we know about that?"

"The main person in Adele White's documentary is said to have lived on a large property up there. According to Robert McCloud, she caused him grief at one stage … so she's some sort of threat; also, she was living on crown land, so the army demolished her place."

"And who found the old Commander guy, sir?" the same voice questioned.

Skip shrugged. "Don't know the full story … do you know, Michael?"

"Yes, I have that report. The team who went up to do a further search of the wreckage captured him after he had attacked two soldiers. Army reconnaissance brought him back here."

"Right … well, it is my hunch that the answers to all these questions can be found up north. I don't know why or how, but that Commander said he belonged to some sort of community and he became lost or separated or something. He was never clear about it, but he certainly possessed some unique abilities." Skip paused, remembering the seconds before McCloud died. He could not forget the violence in the Commander's eyes. That old man had reached a state of madness that was beyond anger and as he shot a look of pure hatred at McCloud, Rob instantly collapsed. It was over in a second. Skip Warner knew the incident was so extreme it could be called evil, but he also knew he would never share it with anyone. "He had abilities that are beyond most of us, and he also referred to us as Earthlings, which was amusing at the time."

"Are you suggesting that he was not from here … that he was some type of alien?" Taft snapped angrily.

"No, Michael, I'm not. No such creature exists but take a note … the Commander had the type of mental power that most of us do not possess. He could read minds, and he had control of some sort of energy that could affect our consciousness." Warner looked around the room. "So … people … be careful. This is a warning. That old man was definitely not like us, and I am sure there are others up there that can give us the same type of problem." Skip turned his attention back to the five men crowding around him. "I have orders to find the powder, to find Adele White, and to try to gather information about Professor Egeland … and I am sure all those answers will be found up there in the north." He paused for a moment, looking around at his team, pleased that he was in charge. One of his motives for creating this operation was to square the account for Rob. It was in retaliation; somebody must pay for his friend's death, but he did not intend to share this with anyone either. "So, tomorrow it starts. We will take thermal imaging devices, dogs, and x-ray equipment, everything we need to find these guys. The army has been up there quite a few times now, but always they've been unsuccessful. This time we will succeed. We'll take control of the powder and lock up these terrorists for good. The Kimberley is our objective, and we leave at first light tomorrow."

Chapter Three
Chaldee's Audience with Isaak

Outside the healing center Isaak suggested that Abe show Ben, Joe, Enka, and Aegeus some of the features of their city, then he turned to Chaldee: "My Lady, I would like it if you came to my rooms, there is much we need to discuss."

Chaldee nodded and followed him down a wide glittering hallway and into a beautifully furnished room. Couches and large chairs were scattered about. The carpet was a delicate creamy-white, the multicolored drapes seemed almost to flow into the walls, and the rich tapestries and paintings gave the entire room an extraordinary feeling of quality.

"Please sit," Isaak instructed. "We must talk."

Chaldee obeyed, looking puzzled.

"I was aware of your people's very sudden and unexpected arrival in the valley, but I do not understand exactly how it happened."

Chaldee smiled. Obviously, Isaak was more aware than she realized. "Many thousands of years ago my ancestors placed our race in a parallel dimension because of the hostilities of a society of Earthlings. These brilliant men left us guidelines via a series of prophesies instructing that at a certain time we would have to realign our world with that of the Earthlings … and we did this not long ago."

"Ah … that makes sense."

"But I feel that you have also spent much time away from your natural environment."

Isaak nodded. "Our ancestry is connected to the Lemurian race. Originally, we came from islands in the Indian Ocean. When the sea swept in and covered them, a few survivors found this land; that was around the same time as I believe your scientists arrived on Earth. I think there was some interaction between our two peoples back then."

"But we are talking around seventy-five thousand years ago, Isaak. Surely that is too long ago to be of any concern."

"Ah! Time! If one considers such a huge time span, I agree that what happened back then matters little to us now, but if one moves out of this third dimension, reality alters, and time ceases to dominate events. You can see under those circumstances the closeness of our two races becomes of great interest … to me anyway."

"I stand corrected."

"No, please … I did not mean to chastise you, Princess Chaldee. I am merely trying to develop a dialogue between us for I am certain that our meeting has been predetermined at some level."

Chaldee stood up and wandered over to a heavy wall tapestry depicting two large odd-looking ships tossed on a wild ocean. "Is this a scene from your past?"

"My grandmother created that wall hanging, and, yes, she was recording one of our many stories, an event of survival."

"So, you believe in the past our two peoples interacted," Chaldee mused as she wandered around the room.

"A very positive meeting from how I read the records that were kept back then. This is why I wanted to speak with you now. It is more than a coincidence that you are looking for a new home, just as some of my people are preparing to leave this realm."

"Leave?"

"Yes. Through many years and many incarnations, they have developed a state of awareness and such a heightened resonance that life on this planet is no longer necessary. Thus, many are ready to transfer their consciousness to another frequency. This is how this wonderful realm of matter creates growth. Our experiences here in this reality, whether they are good or bad, contribute to growth and development."

Chaldee leaned forward, her eyes revealing the intensity of her interest. "That's what we were just speaking about and I find this quite exciting, for it seems that our existence here aids our transition to a higher frequency."

"Exactly so, My Lady. People may seek success, skill, money, love, but these results are gained via experience, and it is the experience that manifests development."

Chaldee smiled, entranced by his words. "My people know this as the creative force: the sacred energy that creates this world of matter … and our experience."

Isaak nodded emphatically. "And as I have mentioned, so many of our people are transitioning that soon this city will be in need of an increase in population."

"And we are looking for a home," Chaldee said, clapping her hands gleefully.

"Exactly. Your arrival has been foretold in our records."

"Really!" Chaldee returned to her chair, staring across at her benefactor, both amazed and grateful. She could feel new energy pouring through her body. Her pain at losing her kingdom plus her terrible lack of direction was suddenly gone.

"But I have to caution you, My Lady. There will be many more Earthlings joining you as the surface of this planet becomes more hostile. Already you have collected a wonderful group of humans and I am sure they will want to bring more of their friends, and so this trickle will eventually become a whirlpool of migration."

Chaldee's eyes opened in surprise. Such an outcome had never crossed her mind, but as Isaak continued, she began to understand some of the later predictions in the sacred scrolls.

"It is written that the union of our two races is inevitable," Chaldee whispered.

"Yes." Isaak nodded. "But I am very aware of the effects this underground lifestyle might have on some of your Earthling friends. I do see a future when many in your community will move here, but there needs to be an interim period, a time of adjustment."

Chaldee frowned, not quite sure what was being said. "But life in this beautiful city would be so peaceful, so uplifting." She stood up, spreading her arms wide. "It is beautiful."

"Ah … maybe for you, Princess Chaldee, but the humans who will join your community will still seek sunlight, they will still want to feel the changing of the seasons and long for wind and rain. These humans are nurtured by the natural world, and they will need time and instruction to make the adjustment."

"So, what are you suggesting, Isaak?"

"I know of a place. In the past many of our own people needed to remain in contact with the surface world, so a small setting was developed. It has not been used for a very long time, but it is nearby so access to this city will not be a problem."

"I am beginning to understand, and I thank you again, Isaak." Chaldee moved to his chair and bent over to kiss the cheek of this very tall, very thin man who seemed at times to almost disappear. "I am so grateful. This entire conversation has brightened my day. I was almost in despair trying to unravel a future for my people, but within minutes you have lifted this weight." Chaldee gently touched his arm. "And I like what you have suggested, the idea of sheltering Earthlings where they will still be in touch with Nature."

"And I thank you, My Lady," Isaak said, raising her hands to his lips. "It is not often that I am given such an opportunity."

Chaldee nodded regally. "As you suggest, this is more than a coincidence."

Isaak smiled knowingly. "Yes, indeed."

There was a comfortable silence in the room, but as Chaldee settled back in her chair, she felt a sudden flood of stressful energy. Startled she looked across at Isaak. "Something is wrong! What has happened!" She stood up in dismay. Then as the Master Speaker's message began to make sense she moaned: "No! This cannot be! Will it never end? Zell is telling me that once again the humans have returned."

Chapter Four
Master Speaker Fights Back

The Master Speaker had left the caves, joining those who were organizing the removal of more furniture from the abandoned houses in the valley. While down there a few men had decided to try to dismantle the buildings so they could use the timber. It was heavy work and the entire group had spent the morning struggling with this task. The wet season's torrential rains had arrived, so it was hot and very sticky. They were all still new to this tropical climate so many had become exhausted.

"We need to rest," the Master Speaker warned. "We must not become overheated."

There was a general agreement. Water and food were handed round but as the group lay back in the shadows of the trees, they realized the brooding sky was becoming dark.

"It will rain again soon," one man warned.

"Yes, it might be better if we packed up," the Master Speaker agreed.

As they began to organize what they had collected during the trip, Zell wandered toward the wreckage of the palace. He had been here a few times since the attack and his grief was as heartbreaking as ever. He felt too old to change, and his memory of the life he had led in Chaldee's palace was brighter than this present life as they tried to eke out a living in those wretched caves. As he pondered his past, wandering through the burned debris, he slowly began to feel a tension in his solar plexus. Momentarily he thought it was because of where he was, but as the feeling grew stronger, he became alert. Calling urgently, he hurried back to the group under the trees. "Everybody … quickly … gather your things, I feel a tremor in the energy around us. We must get back to the cave."

Without a word the whole group obeyed. They knew the Master Speaker had profound abilities, with telepathic skills beyond their own. He had always ruled wisely when Princess Chaldee was away, so they quickly started to clamber back toward the caves, still not sure what was wrong.

Suddenly they heard the faint but familiar sound of helicopters.

"Oh no … once again they are coming in search of our home!" The Master Speaker glanced worriedly at his flock. "Those human machines are almost here … you all must flee … go farther down the valley toward the falls. I will stay here and try to divert them."

"But, Master Speaker, it is too dangerous."

"Go! Do as I say. We have not time to reach the cave but if you all hide farther down the valley this will save you. I must know you are all safe."

For a moment longer they stayed, wanting to help, wanting to run, unsure of what they should do.

"Go, I say … now! I will be all right; I feel it."

Wordlessly they obeyed, and he watched as they disappeared into the thick bush. The sound was growing so he knew that soon he would see the human craft, so he tucked himself behind a large tree and again reached out to Chaldee. She must be told of this terrible event.

In the lead helicopter, Skip Warner was preparing to land. He had not been here before, but the pilot had just given him a thumbs-up, so he realized they were close.

"Again, I must warn you all to be alert. We are moving against an unknown enemy. Others who have come up here have not realized how difficult these people are, but I have seen the damage they can do. This warning is vitally important; you must make sure you keep your helmets on and visors down as we make contact. Okay!"

There was a general murmur of agreement as the police officers readied themselves.

Once both helicopters had landed, Skip was first on the ground, taking charge as the officers and their dogs followed and the rest of the equipment was unloaded.

"We'll set up a base here. Put up the tents so our equipment can be stored, and hurry, there's a storm coming ... make sure ..." Skip's words faded as there was a shout of warning and he turned to see an old man approaching. Momentarily his face drained of color as he thought he was looking at the Commander, then realized that this man was not as tall and was much thinner.

"Visors down," he screamed as he allowed the old man to move closer.

In the darkening gloom as storm clouds pressed onto the land, the Master Speaker watched the helicopters land. He saw two animals that he thought might be similar to the one they called Dog, the animal who had died saving Rod; that was long past, yet his people were still being forced to deal with these aggressive humans. He wiped his face as he remembered. Things were bad back then and nothing had changed. He watched closely as the Earthlings began to unload odd-looking equipment but stayed out of sight a moment longer noting how ferocious the four-legged animals looked. Eventually Zell knew he must make a move, and so he ambled out from behind the tree and slowly approached the landing area. He was still unsure of what he could do, but he was hopeful that his people had moved far enough away to be safe. Chaldee had not yet answered his call for help, so stalling for time, he said: "I bid you welcome … all of you."

"No … no … no … Everybody … keep your visors down!"

The man who appeared to be the leader was now yelling garbled words in a high-pitched but furious voice. He sounded like a madman but then Zell realized that this human was holding one of those deadly little weapons, and it was pointed straight at him.

"You just keep your distance, mate, and don't try that welcome rubbish with me." As he spoke, the hysterical officer waved the weapon wildly.

"You are visitors here; this is why I offer you an invitation to our land."

"Did you know the Commander?" The man with the gun stuttered slightly then took a step closer. "Was he from here, too?"

The Master Speaker felt a jolt of surprise. So, these were the people who had taken the Commander. "Yes," he said slowly. "He is known to me."

"Well, my friend, your mate is dead, so I advise you to take care."

Zell stumbled as he heard this news. He had often had bitter arguments with the Commander, but never would he have wished the man such a fate, so this news was horrifying. Such brutality, killing the Commander and boasting about it. The Master Speaker chastised himself as he admitted that this was a silly thing he was doing, facing these dangerous Earthlings without any type of defense. He took a deep breath. He must not be reckless. And as he tried to calm himself, Zell stared at the human in front of him, carefully reading his thoughts. It would seem that this man was determined to find the Princess and Adele. The Master Speaker frowned inwardly, wondering why they would want Adele. As he tried to gain more information, he realized that the talk of the Commander's death was not important to these humans. It was being used as a tool to cause him fear. Zell drew a sharp breath; well, that tactic was certainly working.

"I am saddened by such news. How did he die?" As he spoke, the Master Speaker scanned the thoughts of the other officers. All were alert and anxious. They were certainly ready to attack if ordered so he knew he must not appear confrontational or aggressive.

"The Commander is of no importance, we are here to collect the material Professor Egeland developed, so tell your princess lady, or whoever she claims she is, to hand over the powder."

The sudden sound of thunder rolled around the valley, its violence blocking Skip's words, so the Master Speaker shrugged slightly, claiming softly: "I know nothing of Professor Egeland's work."

Skip Warner took a step closer and the Master Speaker could see the small weapon was still pointing at him. "Is this woman your boss?"

"She is our reigning monarch, sir." The Master Speaker looked closely into the mind of this aggressor. He seemed a very nervous man. Almost as frightened as he himself was. It seemed this human had witnessed some terrible act the Commander had performed and was now almost rigid with fear, expecting the same type of attack.

"Well, she's the one we want."

As the Master Speaker's mind whirled, trying

to think of his next move, there was another shattering roll of thunder, then one of Skip's officers gave a yell of excitement. "Sir, I think I saw a movement farther down the valley." The officer who was speaking seemed impervious to the weather. "Shall I take the dogs, sir?"

The warm tropical air thickened as it began to rain. Within seconds, this became a downpour and for a moment, as Zell stood in the deluge, he considered running but he knew he could not. His duty was here, trying to stop any further invasion of their lands, but then his heart dropped as he saw Skip squinting through the rain-sodden darkness staring in the direction the officer was pointing. Obviously, they had seen one of his people.

Zell tried to speak but was silenced by the storm. Then he heard Skip yell: "Take Schultz with you, but be careful, these guys are dangerous."

As the rain flooded across the area, turning the palace wreckage to ugly mud, the Master Speaker felt another spark of fear. They had unchained the dogs. These animals had been cooped up for hours and were so eager to run they almost pulled the officers over. Despite the storm and despite the men trying to keep control, the dogs were free. As he watched, Zell realized what a fearsome enemy was being let loose on his people. As they disappeared through the sheets of rain, the Master Speaker's heart and mind became numb; he began to admit that there really was no hope. How could his people stand up against these Earthlings? But suddenly his whole being became alert. He could hear Chaldee's welcome voice ringing in his head, telling him to stay calm. Was this really her? She was telling him that help was on the way. He staggered against a tree as a feeling of relief lifted his panic.

Annoyingly, at the same moment, the leading officer's voice broke across the Master Speaker's inner focus, barking out an order: "Okay, mister, it's time I met this woman you call a leader." As he spoke, the Earthling roughly grabbed at the Master Speaker's arm, and without thinking Zell pierced an angry stare at his attacker. Even though Skip Warner had his visor down, Zell's energy was still powerful enough to cause him to lose consciousness and collapse into the mud.

Instinctively the officer standing beside Skip fired a warning shot in the air, yelling at the Master Speaker to stand down, but Zell was now beyond fear. He saw that although he had crippled the Earthling leader he was again being threatened.

"Would you dare to shoot … you mindless Earthling," he snarled, taking a step closer. As he moved, the Master Speaker realized the man pointing the gun was almost frozen with fear, so he speared him with another probing stare but as this man pitched forward the Master Speaker himself was hit from behind with such a sharp blow he fell to his knees. As he tried to steady himself—blood pouring from a deep head wound—Zell heard Chaldee's voice again, telling him to be strong, that Isaak was coming.

The Master Speaker sat heavily on the ground, listening to her promise, wiping the blood from his face, and staring up at his attacker. "You must desist from this nonsense," he said weakly. "You do not know who you are fighting."

"I agree … these aggressive tactics are useless." This eerie, unseen voice seemed full of dark menace to all those who heard it.

The Master Speaker realized that it was Isaak, but the remaining police officer and the two pilots had no idea of what they had just heard. These strange words seem to reach over the sound of the rain and totally unnerved the three humans as they frantically huddled together close to one of the helicopters. He could see that they had instinctively reached out to the solid reality of the craft. It was the only thing to focus on and the Master Speaker realized that the machine's concrete reality was keeping them from losing control.

"… and you are not welcome here." As he heard Isaak's warning, Zell saw a soft light beginning to form, then inside this glow Isaak's body began to take shape. The Master Speaker fell back in relief. He did not notice the terror on the faces of the three humans but as Isaak's physical shape emerged, small gasps of horror could be heard coming from these professional men. They were being forced to deal with something unknown and unidentified; the type of apparition they thought belonged in children's books was slowly taking shape before them and they stared in total disbelief. One pilot was so alarmed he had to turn away, pressing his face against the metal craft as the solid world that he had known all his life seemed to be crumbling around him.

Although Zell was overcome by gratitude, his head was hurting too much to stand so from his position on the ground he saw Isaak taking control. The men were huddled together as this thin wavering figure instructed them to pick up those who were unconscious and put them into the machine.

As this began to happen, the rain also began to ease. Now completely wet, with blood seeping into his eyes, the old Master Speaker weakly warned Isaak to beware of the dogs and the other two officers.

The sound of gunfire had caused these men to return, but their attitude of bravado quickly faded into fear as they saw Isaak's form fading away, returning, then fading again. Now they meekly obeyed his instructions and within a few minutes the entire team had been pushed into one machine. Isaak again warned them that they were trespassing; that they must leave and not return. In fact, Isaak's last warning confounded Zell, for this tall, willowy being was telling the Earthlings that all human combat forces were now off-limits; that there was no way anybody would ever be able to land here again.

The Master Speaker watched as the helicopter began to lift off the ground. It was hard to believe that a situation that had seemed like annihilation ten minutes ago was suddenly resolved.

After the machine had disappeared, Isaak drifted across to where the Master Speaker sat, trying to ease the trickle of blood. "That wound needs attention, sir."

The Master Speaker nodded. "Yes … it will be fine soon … but I thank you, Isaak, your help has saved my people."

Isaak assisted the old man to his feet. "Yes, those scoundrels have gone, but we must stop any of them from returning."

"I heard you say this … but how?"

Isaak smiled and produced a hand full of small crystals. "These are very powerful. They will set up a magnetic force that will confuse any navigational system."

"Ah … I see. Some type of magnetics."

"That is close enough." Isaak smiled. "Any aircraft system aiming at this area will be restricted by the frequency of these crystals."

"How will we use them, though? We know nothing of such science."

Isaak smiled again, his whole being wavering as he began to glide across the ground. "I will place these crystals in strategic places. They will align with the Earth's natural magnetic force. The valley will become completely hidden from all guidance systems." Isaak paused thoughtfully as he surveyed the area. "And anyway, I'm sure this area will eventually flood. That tiny stream trickling through the rockslide is becoming quite a river and by the end of the wet season this valley will be under water."

The Master Speaker was surprised. Such an event had not crossed his mind. "You mean a river will flow through here?"

"Yes. Eventually all remnants of the destruction that took place here will be washed away." Isaak touched the Master Speaker's bloody head. "It does not seem too bad now the bleeding has stopped."

Unconcerned by his wound, Zell queried: "So you are saying that this area that once was Princess Chaldee's palace will be under water." Carefully he pondered this new information and it pleased him. "Sir, I think such an outcome is perfect."

"I understand completely," Isaak said. "But now I must assess the area so I can strategically place these crystals where they will cause the most disturbance." He laughed loudly. "Meanwhile, I suggest you use some of your powder on that wound."

As he spoke, Isaak's image began to fade. "That powder is magical and will be of much help to all of us in the future." Now Isaak seemed to be speaking from an invisible world. The Master Speaker smiled at the magical quality of Isaak's reality, as he stared at where Isaak had been, then with a deep sigh of satisfaction he lay back, waiting for his people to arrive.

Chapter Five
The Discovery of Their New Home

Isaak had placed the tiny crystals in strategic places around the valley and had returned to the inner-Earth city, describing with much laughter the effect his appearance had had on the Earthling officers. They listened, quite amazed by his account, seeing through his eyes and laughing helplessly, but Chaldee knew that Zell would have quite a different story to tell. He would have been shocked, perhaps even traumatized, and this meant she must return to the caves immediately. Also, she was concerned about Adele, for the Master Speaker had sent a short communication indicating that Adele appeared almost too weak to stand.

"Isaak, I thank you for everything, but I must return to the cave. There is much to be done there."

"And what about the special area I mentioned, where newcomers to this reality can have both cave shelter and open land? Can someone reopen that section?"

"Yes. Of course." Chaldee turned to Paul. "Have you spoken with Isaak about this place?"

Paul nodded.

"You are much improved, so within another day or so I think you might be able to resume your exploration,"

Isaak said with a broad smile. "I can see how eager you are."

Paul grinned. "I feel fantastic. I have no idea what you guys have done, but really I feel amazing."

"Aegeus claims the professor's material can interact with one's consciousness, and this is what Joe used on your wounds."

Paul shook his head, a little unsure. "All that is a bit beyond my pay grade, I'm afraid, but it certainly has helped me."

"Of course," Isaak agreed.

"But anyway, I feel great."

"Then you would be happy to take Joe, Ben, and Jake with you on your search?" Isaak asked.

"I think Enka would also like to be part of this," Chaldee said quickly. "He and Joe have become dear friends."

Both Paul and Isaak smiled in agreement.

"Then I will get ready to return to the caves," Chaldee said quietly. "But I think Aegeus wants to stay here a little longer as there is much to investigate in your city."

"He is most welcome."

"If someone can find Patch for me, he will lead me back."

"Excellent." Isaak bent and kissed Chaldee's cheek. "I am so pleased we are to become neighbors."

Gingerly, Paul stood up, taking Chaldee by both shoulders. "Thanks," he whispered as he bent and kissed her. "You know … being here and having quite a few intense talks with Abe has given me more of an insight into your world." He pulled her close. "Something has changed, Chaldee. I don't really understand."

Chaldee frowned a little as she stared up into his face.

"There's so much I must explain," he whispered.

For a brief moment Chaldee felt surprised then as she scanned his innermost thoughts, she realized what he was saying. “I can see what you mean.” Chaldee slipped her arms around his neck. “And I am overwhelmed.”

Paul nodded and still holding Chaldee he turned to Isaak. “I must thank you so much!”

Isaak bent and kissed each of them on the forehead. “You both will make your mark here in the future.”

For a moment Paul and Chaldee were caught up in the power of their feelings. There was such a bright energy surrounding them that Chaldee was reluctant to break away.

Eventually she murmured: “Patch can help me with the journey back to the caves.”

“I’m missing you already.” Paul smiled, pretending to wipe away tears.

“And I you!” Tenderly she held Paul’s face in her hands. Her feelings had become so strong that Chaldee found them hard to deal with. They were both joyous and fearful at the same time. She kissed him deeply before pulling away. “I must go.”

Chaldee found Patch waiting for her at the door and reluctantly she left.

Soon Paul was telling anyone who would listen how well he felt, so they began to plan their journey out into the area Isaak claimed was ideal for their new home. Abe had a vague idea of the route, but Paul insisted they draw a map that included both Chaldee’s caves, and the city, so he had a clear picture in his head.

Abe pleaded that he be part of the exploration, too, so eventually the six men left the city, equipped with heavy ropes, lights, helmets, and protective clothing. When they crossed the ramp that led back into the tunnel system, Abe automatically began to lead. "We need to backtrack to where that rim runs around the edge of the gorge."

"I think that gorge is really another cave," Joe said thoughtfully. "We had reached this point originally."

"Did we? I don't remember."

Joe smiled. "I'm not surprised, Paul. Anyway, from that ledge down to the cave floor I estimate it's about a thirty-foot drop."

"Okay, that's not a problem," Abe nodded. "If I remember … that rim is actually quite a wide ledge and I think the place we are looking for is on the other side."

Joe was feeling uneasy. "I am not sure how safe it is."

"We'll test it, that's for sure," Paul said tersely. "I don't want another fall."

As they reached the juncture where one section of the tunnel turned sharply and began to circle around what they had thought was a type of gorge, it became apparent that below them was another cave.

Paul called a halt. "We have to test this ledge. It does not look safe to me."

"I'm the lightest," Abe laughed. "Plus falling is not something I worry about."

"Yeah, but that's not what we want," Jake said, refusing to see what Abe thought was funny. "We need weight … somebody who can put pressure on it … somebody like me."

Paul cocked his head on one side, looking hesitantly at his friend.

"You know I'm right."

Paul nodded. "Okay, get the harness and ropes. We'll do this very carefully."

They helped Jake into the safety harness, and he began to crawl out along the ledge, carefully testing its stability, but he was only a short way along the rim when ahead he could see that the ledge had crumbled. "It's no good, I'm afraid," Jake called as he began to inch backward, but as he did, he felt the ground shudder. "Hey! It's going …" he yelled as the ledge broke away and he found himself swinging in midair.

Quickly they winched him back to safety.

"Well, that's a bit of a blow," Ben mused.

"Are you sure this is the right way, Abe?"

Abe looked around at the worried faces and laughed. "Don't look so miserable … let me explore a little."

They all watched, still a little unnerved by Abe's ability to shift his physical form through dimensions but when he had disappeared Jake leaned over the edge staring down into the darkness. "So … what'd ya reckon?"

"Well, we are going to have to abseil down there … that's if that's where we should be going."

Paul nodded at Enka's suggestion. "But let's wait till Abe gets back."

The five of them lined the edge of the ledge, waiting, staring out into the darkness of this unknown void, each one aware of the difficulty suddenly facing them. This was not going to be easy.

Within a few minutes Abe appeared again. "We are at the top of a large cave system. There's a small river running through the center and from what I could see, there seems to be an easier path leading upward from the base on the other side."

"I guess Jake's right … we'll have to do a bit of abseiling."

"Great," Ben muttered. "Just what I need."

"You'll be fine, mate." Paul laughed, patting him on the back.

"I saw the remnants of a foot bridge hanging from the ledge opposite," Abe continued. "So, I think that was how they used to cross over … but we will have to climb back up the other side."

"But you are sure it's the right way?" Jake asked, still sounding doubtful.

"I am certain, Jake, my friend … certain," Abe teased, laughing at Jake's misery.

"Okay, let's gear up. We'll go one at a time." Paul was already sorting through the ropes as he spoke.

"And I'll watch," Ben said firmly. "I'll stay here, and you guys can pick me up on the way back."

"No!" Paul was alarmed. "We must stay together … you'll be fine, Ben."

"Just watch," Enka said kindly. "There really is nothing to it."

"And the fall is only around twenty to thirty feet," Abe reassured the fearful pilot.

Each man moved carefully down the rockface, so eventually there was enough light beaming around the cave below for Ben to see the bottom quite clearly. Nevertheless, even as Paul helped him, Ben was still awkward, bumping and sliding as he tumbled down the side of the cliff.

Once Paul was sure everybody was down and safe, he quickly abseiled across the rough terrain leaving the gear in place ready for the return trip.

As the team shone their lights around the massive cave, they were impressed by the size and the strange beauty of the place. Huge boulders were humped strangely, laying together around the center of the cave, while rivulets of water pooled across the rocks. There were a few stalagmites rising up from the cave floor and scattered everywhere were tiny pockets of exquisite cave pearls. Nevertheless, because of its size most of the cave remained blanketed in darkness, with the beams of their helmets throwing strange moving shapes across the emptiness.

As Abe splashed through the shallow stream, Paul

realized that as the wet season continued this water might become quite deep, so his mind went back to the broken rope ladder Abe mentioned. If this was the way Chaldee's people had to come, they would need to repair this swing bridge, but because that problem was not of prime concern right now, he pushed it aside. The team would deal with that later.

With Abe leading, the group found the climb up the opposite wall much easier and it led into a type of top story of the cave below.

"Seems there are quite a few levels to these caves," Joe called as they carefully moved across the rough floor.

"It's certainly quite a complex system," Paul agreed.

Gradually the roof of this cave sloped down until they found themselves almost crouching.

"Watch out for snakes," Enka warned. "I feel we are encroaching on their world."

He got grunts in return as they slowly pushed forward and so with a great deal of crawling and wriggling, they eventually forced their way through a small opening, finding themselves in another huge, silent cave, but this time there was light. In the far distance they could see how shafts of hazy sunlight were attacking the darkness. With a sudden spurt of energy, the group moved toward the light.

"We're getting close," Jake puffed as they were stopped again, this time by a mass of bushy undergrowth blocking the cave entrance.

Paul was the first to hack his way through. He shielded his eyes from the blinding sun as he stepped out into a landscape that almost seemed like a dream. The others followed and there were gasps of amazement. In front of them was a very large, flat, grassy plateau and beyond that the land sloped away. The entire vista was ringed on three sides by a high rocky ridge forming a horseshoe-shaped amphitheater. Beyond that, through what looked to be a man-made gateway, they could see that the slope became a steep hill running down to a small stream cutting through the rocks. The whole area was covered in low bushy grassland and spindly trees, but Joe could see some very large boab trees growing up against the rocky escarpment and a couple of lush Kakadu plum trees dotted farther down the slope.

"There's water down there at the bottom of that gully," Joe said quietly. "I think this place might be perfect!"

"It's untouched." Paul shook his head in amazement.

"It's beautiful," Enka said as he moved out of the shade of the cave. "But it's very hot."

"Yeah … but maybe farther down the hill it'll be cooler," Joe suggested as he walked out into the center of the grassland.

The men gazed around at how the lush, open land was protected by a mountainous ridge of rock.

"It's a perfect sanctuary."

"Absolutely! Nobody would ever know this was here," Paul said at last. "But there's a lot to explore here. I think it'll take days."

"But it's perfect for us," Enka whispered, bewildered by the improbable scene before him. "It's so perfect I feel it is meant to be."

"I'm not sure who used it in the past … but Isaak can tell you its history," Abe assured them. "I know it was a haven for people for thousands of years, but it's not been used in my lifetime."

"This is some place!" Paul sat down at the cave entrance, leaning back so he felt comfortable. "I think we have found our new home," he said as he stared out at its untouched perfection.

Chapter Six
A Promising Future

Adele was still feeling drained, and emotionally exhausted, so when the exploration team got back, excitedly crowding into the cave talking over each other as they described the hidden retreat and how it could become a new safe haven, Adele moved away, not able to deal with the noise. They seemed victorious about what they had found, full of plans and talking about future trips, but Adele could not feel their excitement. Silently she faded into the background, sad yet relieved that she did not have to share such enthusiasm.

Eventually Jake found her, but she knew he could see she was not much brighter. When he quietly asked how she was feeling, his eyes were silently begging for much more. With great effort she tried to calm him, hiding her aching loss behind a weak smile.

Eventually, after a happy meal, with a great deal of noisy chatter, Adele again found the crowded cave overwhelming. Unable to keep up her pretense, Adele asked Jake to join her and they slowly wandered down into the valley. Almost as soon as she was out in the oppressive heat, Adele realized how weak she had become. So, with Jake's support, they moved across to where a small stream was winding its way through the trees.

"You must try to eat, Adele; I can see that you are

losing strength."

Adele nodded but did not answer.

"Chaldee is worried about you, too."

Adele smoothed the leaves off a tree stump and sat down.

"Adele, do you realize how concerned we are?"

"I'm okay, Jake," Adele whispered. "I just need to rest."

Jake sat on the ground in front of her, staring up. "I'm afraid we have to leave tomorrow. Ben's got some sort of job he cannot get out of."

"Of course, you must go."

"It's too dangerous for you to come, but I need to know you're okay."

Silently, Adele stared across to where the water was winding down through the valley.

"I hate to leave you like this."

"Jake, there is no 'us' anymore." She could see that he was stunned although he did not speak. "I'm sorry but I feel I'm on my own; the trouble is nothing I do … or anyone does … seems important anymore."

"It's just the misery talking, sweetheart. You have to grieve. I know that, but one day things will seem brighter … trust me."

Adele shrugged but did not answer.

"We can't let it go like this," Jake protested.

"It's odd," she whispered. "It's been over between us for quite a while, but we just didn't realize."

Jake was shaking his head.

"And you're right … I'm sad about Dad. In fact, more than sad … I'm devastated." She paused, trying to get her breath. "I can't believe he's gone … but what is happening here now is about us, Jake. Fundamentally I have changed. Over the past twelve months I have felt some type of enormous shift taking place, yet you really haven't noticed. It's because of who you are and who I am. It's not wrong or right, it just is."

"It's about your dad ..."

"No, it isn't, Jake, it's me. It's being here. I know you can't see this. You live in a different world, one I used to live in, too, Jake, but everything has changed, and now with Dad dying, I just need space ... time to find out who I really am."

Jake stood up and wandered down to the water's edge unaware that Chaldee was making her way toward them.

"Adele, are you all right?" Chaldee stood looking down at Adele. "Paul and I have been worried."

"I'm tired, I'm sad, but I'll be okay, Chaldee."

"She's not all right," Jake called.

Chaldee looked at them both, and Adele knew that Chaldee understood the conflict, perhaps even better than she did herself. "Try and explain it to him, Chaldee. Tell him that people change, that people grow apart, that nothing in this world stays the same ... tell him," Adele muttered sadly.

Jake came back and stood with Chaldee. "You used to be outrageous and funny, Adele. I mean ... you used to challenge me all the time." Jake paused scratching his ear. "I need to understand it. Why do you say you are different?"

Adele stood up and put her arms around him. "We've just grown apart, that's all."

Jake clung to her, and she could feel that he was slowly being forced to recognize that something was indeed different.

"You will continue to do what you do best. You fight, you resist, you want the world to change ... well, I have. Maybe this is where it all starts? With each of us!" Adele kissed him lightly and stepped back.

He shook his head. "What you're saying is too much for me to deal with right now. We're going back tomorrow, and things might become a bit threatening."

"I realize … and I'm sorry, Jake, I really am," Adele said tearfully, wiping her face with the back of her hand. "I still care … but it's different now. I can't explain, and I hate hurting you like this."

With a bitter shrug, Jake walked away, heading back up to the cave.

Chaldee took Adele's hand, but said nothing as they watched Jake disappear.

Chaldee was pleased that Isaak was standing next to her as she began to explain to her people the wonders of Isaak's city and the opportunity they had suddenly been given. "I am so pleased to be able to tell you that we have two choices as to where we shall live. Isaak's beautiful city awaits anybody who wishes to live there. Soon you all will be able to experience its wonder. Also, we have the opportunity to build a new village on land that is secure, well hidden, yet still above ground. It has the backing of a cave system in case the climate becomes too unstable. Both these places are now awaiting us. This gives us many choices, choices that have been missing from our lives for a long time."

There was a murmur of approval as Chaldee turned to Paul, who was sitting among the crowd. "Could you tell us a little more about the cave system you have explored, Paul?"

Paul stood, then bowing slightly toward Chaldee he began to outline the choices. His action was not missed by those watching. They knew that this was not subservience, rather he was paying homage to their leader. Paul smiled slightly before turning back to this group of people, and

Chaldee realized that he was aware that one day they would accept him.

"There will be a lot of work ahead, I'm afraid, but we have time to do it. There is no need to rush. We will have to widen the passageways leading to this new area which sits on a beautiful plateau probably about two to three hours from here. Isaak's city is a fair distance farther on, but once we clear the route, I am sure movement will become quite easy. We also have to build a swing bridge, but I have been told by Isaak that because his people are not restricted by the limits of third dimension, they will help us with a great deal of the building."

There was a scattering of laughter for it was amusing that Isaak's people, so wondrously able to move through the layers of consciousness, were willing to help with all the construction.

As Chaldee sat watching, she realized that the idea of such a transformation was inspiring to many of her people. They seemed excited by the opportunities that lay ahead. This had been prophesied, and she was now witnessing the full meaning of what had been written. She was gratified by the opportunities that were unfolding for her people. Smiling to herself, she dragged her attention back to the meeting. "The other thing we need to do quickly, is to remove anything we feel we need from the old village site. As the rains continue the whole area will become a river."

"I will organize another scrounge party, Your Highness," the Master Speaker said, smiling at his own invention.

"Scrounge party? I like that term," Isaak teased admiringly.

"Also remember … tomorrow Jake and Ben will leave," Paul reminded everybody.

"Yes," Isaak said quickly: "And I am hoping that part of their mission will be to find any Earthling who supports the idea of a new beginning. This is what we can offer them. A safe place to start anew."

"Absolutely, Isaak, and I am sure there will be quite a few who will want to come," Ben said. "We will take my chopper and the one the police left behind can be used as a spare … maybe Paul will eventually fly, too, then he can help if enough people want to join us up here." Ben smiled at Paul. "A few more lessons and you'll be good to go."

"Well, let us adjourn for now, but please ask Isaak as many questions as you wish for his city is a place many of you will love." Chaldee smiled and quietly moved across to her private quarters. She had much to consider.

Although Chaldee was excited by the new prospects that awaited her people, and the promising change she could feel in Paul's attitude, she was also very concerned by Adele's state of mind. She searched the cave and the area beyond but the girl was missing. Frowning a little Chaldee began to look for Jake, but he had also disappeared. Standing in the darkness, staring out into the night, Chaldee was suddenly hopeful that they might be able to sort out their differences. Jake was leaving in the morning, so there was still time.

The next morning Ben and Jake left early, promising to be back in a month. There was no sign of Adele as everybody mingled around Ben's machine, and Chaldee could see that Jake did not appear troubled, so she was hopeful that they had worked through some of their differences.

Ben assured Paul that next time he was up they would work on Paul's flying skills, and Joe laughingly said he doubted such a miracle would come to pass. Eventually the four friends briefly hugged, not wanting to say good-bye.

Nothing was certain, not in these days of crisis, so Chaldee realized there was a chance they might never return. Nevertheless, as she watched the small craft vanish into the clouds, she refused to take such a negative thought any further. Also, she wished that Jake and Adele could be happy. The heart had enormous power to change a person so maybe they did have a future. She looked across at Paul, and knew that he, too, was changing, but in an exciting way. Something had happened as he recovered from his fall. Perhaps it was the effect of the powder, or maybe it was being with Abe and Isaak, she was not sure, but Paul was different. Lasting relationships demanded harmony and deep understanding, and she felt that maybe she and Paul were working toward such a state.

The Master Speaker stood next to Chaldee as they watched the helicopter vanish. He realized that there was still much that needed to be done, but they had overcome most of their problems. Indeed, the future looked very promising. As he monitored Chaldee's thoughts, he realized how happy she was, and this was the most pleasing of all. As he stood surveying the sky, the valley, and his people, he realized that very soon he and the other elders of the kingdom would be asked to consider Princess Chaldee's marriage.

About the Author

Lyn Willmott has a BA in Ceramic Design, and another in teaching. She has run her own pottery business and has taught Art and English expression in a variety of class rooms – including five years where she ran the education department in a prison. At the age of sixty she became a fitness instructor and has helped conduct fitness trials for the aged. She has written 2 science fiction/fantasy novels for young adults and numerous short stories.

Books by Lyn Willmott

A Small Book of Comfort
Published by: Ozark Mountain Publishing

Beyond all Boundaries Book 1
Published by: Big Sandy Press

Beyond all Boundaries Book 2
Published by: Big Sandy Press

For more information about any of the above titles, soon to be released titles, or other items in our catalog, write, phone or visit our website:
Ozark Mountain Publishing, Inc.
PO Box 754, Huntsville, AR 72740
479-738-2348/800-935-0045
www.ozarkmt.com

For more information about any of the titles published by Ozark Mountain Publishing, Inc., soon to be released titles, or other items in our catalog, write, phone or visit our website:

Ozark Mountain Publishing, Inc.

PO Box 754

Huntsville, AR 72740

479-738-2348/800-935-0045

www.ozarkmt.com

If you liked this book, you might also like:

Dancing with Angels in Heaven
by Garnet Schulhauser
Croton, Croton II
By Artur Tadevosyan
The Forgiveness Workshop
by Cat Baldwin
The Oracle of UR
by Penny Barron
The Birthmark Scar
by P.E. Berg & Amanda Hemmingsen
Life As A Military Psychologist
by Sally Wolf

For more information about any of the above titles, soon to be released titles, or other items in our catalog, write, phone or visit our website:
Ozark Mountain Publishing, LLC
PO Box 754, Huntsville, AR 72740
479-738-2348
www.ozarkmt.com

Other Books by Ozark Mountain Publishing, Inc.

Dolores Cannon
A Soul Remembers Hiroshima
Between Death and Life
Conversations with Nostradamus, Volume I, II, III
The Convoluted Universe -Book One, Two, Three, Four, Five
The Custodians
Five Lives Remembered
Jesus and the Essenes
Keepers of the Garden
Legacy from the Stars
The Legend of Starcrash
The Search for Hidden Sacred Knowledge
They Walked with Jesus
The Three Waves of Volunteers and the New Earth
A Vey Special Friend
Aron Abrahamsen
Holiday in Heaven
James Ream Adams
Little Steps
Justine Alessi & M. E. McMillan
Rebirth of the Oracle
Kathryn Andries
Time: The Second Secret
Cat Baldwin
Divine Gifts of Healing
The Forgiveness Workshop
Penny Barron
The Oracle of UR
P.E. Berg & Amanda Hemmingsen
The Birthmark Scar
Dan Bird
Finding Your Way in the Spiritual Age
Waking Up in the Spiritual Age
Julia Cannon
Soul Speak – The Language of Your Body
Ronald Chapman
Seeing True
Jack Churchward
Lifting the Veil on the Lost Continent of Mu
The Stone Tablets of Mu
Patrick De Haan
The Alien Handbook
Paulinne Delcour-Min
Spiritual Gold
Holly Ice
Divine Fire
Joanne DiMaggio
Edgar Cayce and the Unfulfilled Destiny of Thomas Jefferson Reborn
Anthony DeNino
The Power of Giving and Gratitude
Carolyn Greer Daly
Opening to Fullness of Spirit
Anita Holmes
Twidders
Aaron Hoopes
Reconnecting to the Earth
Patricia Irvine
In Light and In Shade
Kevin Killen
Ghosts and Me
Donna Lynn
From Fear to Love
Curt Melliger
Heaven Here on Earth
Where the Weeds Grow
Henry Michaelson
And Jesus Said – A Conversation
Andy Myers
Not Your Average Angel Book
Guy Needler
Avoiding Karma
Beyond the Source – Book 1, Book 2
The History of God
The Origin Speaks

For more information about any of the above titles, soon to be released titles, or other items in our catalog, write, phone or visit our website:
PO Box 754, Huntsville, AR 72740|479-738-2348/800-935-0045|www.ozarkmt.com

Other Books by Ozark Mountain Publishing, Inc.

The Anne Dialogues
The Curators
Psycho Spiritual Healing
James Nussbaumer
And Then I Knew My Abundance
The Master of Everything
Mastering Your Own Spiritual Freedom
Living Your Dram, Not Someone Else's
Sherry O'Brian
Peaks and Valley's
Gabrielle Orr
Akashic Records: One True Love
Let Miracles Happen
Nikki Pattillo
Children of the Stars
A Golden Compass
Victoria Pendragon
Sleep Magic
The Sleeping Phoenix
Being In A Body
Alexander Quinn
Starseeds What's It All About
Charmian Redwood
A New Earth Rising
Coming Home to Lemuria
Richard Rowe
Imagining the Unimaginable
Exploring the Divine Library
Garnet Schulhauser
Dancing on a Stamp
Dancing Forever with Spirit
Dance of Heavenly Bliss
Dance of Eternal Rapture
Dancing with Angels in Heaven
Manuella Stoerzer
Headless Chicken
Annie Stillwater Gray
Education of a Guardian Angel
The Dawn Book
Work of a Guardian Angel
Joys of a Guardian Angel
Blair Styra
Don't Change the Channel
Who Catharted
Natalie Sudman
Application of Impossible Things
L.R. Sumpter
Judy's Story
The Old is New
We Are the Creators
Artur Tradevosyan
Croton
Croton II
Jim Thomas
Tales from the Trance
Jolene and Jason Tierney
A Quest of Transcendence
Paul Travers
Dancing with the Mountains
Nicholas Vesey
Living the Life-Force
Dennis Wheatley/ Maria Wheatley
The Essential Dowsing Guide
Maria Wheatley
Druidic Soul Star Astrology
Sherry Wilde
The Forgotten Promise
Lyn Willmott
A Small Book of Comfort
Beyond all Boundaries Book 1
Beyond all Boundaries Book 2
Beyond all Boundaries Book 3
Stuart Wilson & Joanna Prentis
Atlantis and the New Consciousness
Beyond Limitations
The Essenes -Children of the Light
The Magdalene Version
Power of the Magdalene
Sally Wolf
Life of a Military Psychologist

For more information about any of the above titles, soon to be released titles, or other items in our catalog, write, phone or visit our website:
PO Box 754, Huntsville, AR 72740|479-738-2348/800-935-0045|www.ozarkmt.com